Praise

'Clover C

'This book is for incurable romantics, I couldn't put it down. I want to start the next book in the series right now!'

'Idyllic. I love this magical town with its delightful residents. A visit with these folks is always a nice place to go.'

'I absolutely loved this book: the setting, the characters, the storyline. I am in love with Clover Cove and you will love it too.'

'I got totally lost in this ripping romance. Immediately transported to the gorgeous Emerald Isle and the quirky residents of Clover Cove, I finished the story in record time, wishing I was part of the Cove community. Can't wait to go back for another visit.'

'Heartwarming doesn't come close! Simple loves stories intertwined with insightful gems of wisdom about life, love and family. Clover Cove feels more like home with every new book.'

'Love, love, love this series!'

This edition published by Sunflower & Co 2022

ISBN 978-1-911297-26-0

Also in this series:
A Secret in Clover Cove
The Little Café at Clover Cove
Snow Falls in Clover Cove
A Love Letter to Clover Cove
Coming Home to Clover Cove

maggie-finn.com

Love Comes To Clover Cove

Maggie Finn

Sunflower & Co

Chapter 1

Connor James leant against the ancient chapel and sighed. *Ah, but isn't that pretty?* He thought. Up here on the cliff top, it was the perfect place to view the sunset rippling purple and blue across the Cove. The wind was picking up, ruffling his dark hair, but Connor didn't mind; you couldn't grow up on the west coast of Ireland and complain about the weather. Of course, he smiled, that didn't stop people from trying.

He turned back towards the little village, the tumble of whitewashed cottages turning golden in the sinking sun. The stone church with its curious round tower, the cafe and the post office, their orange lights just flicking on; and the pub. *Connor's.* His pub. The heart of the village, the very place he had been born, his home. And yet right now, Connor felt as far from all of it as he ever had.

Reluctantly, he felt inside his coat, pulling out the half-dozen envelopes he'd grabbed from the kitchen table on the way out. Bills, bills, one or two in glaring, clanging red: Connor didn't need to open them, he knew exactly what they would say. And then the last one: a pale pink envelope, curled, neat handwriting in royal blue ink. Connor could guess what was inside this one too – and he wasn't alone. Orla, the post mistress, had raised her eyebrows to him as she had handed it over. That was the gift and curse of Clover Cove, where no one's affairs were their own, even – particularly – affairs of the heart. Connor felt sure Orla would tell Mary in the church who would tell Molly in the cafe and by the end of the day, half the county would have heard about 'Connor's letter'.

He looked down at it, feeling the texture of the stiff paper. Good quality: but of course it would be. Ciara had always loved the best things in life. He rubbed a thumb over the stamp: the Queen's head, always looking to the left. At least Her Majesty was smart enough to avert her eyes.

And what about you, Con? He thought. *Are you smart too?* It certainly didn't feel that way. The stone sitting on his chest, as dark and heavy as any of the boulders tumbling down below him to the beach, suggested quite the opposite. And he'd been carrying that weight for years now.

Connor closed his eyes and took a deep breath, allowing Ciara's face to swim into view. Those happy days in the meadows high on the cliffs, the walks on the warm sand, the nights wrapped in a blanket watching the stars. Everything had seemed fresh, everything scented with green, just one long hazy summer day.

And it had been grand, hadn't it?

He felt back into his pocket and pulled out his grandfather's old brass lighter and flipped the wheel. For a moment, he watched the flame guttering in the breeze, then the envelope caught and blue fire licked up the paper, the carefully inked address turning grey then black. Just before it scorched his fingers, Connor held it out, then let it go, watching as the last remains of the letter dropped over the edge of the cliff and disappeared into the sea.

'Goodbye my love,' he whispered. 'Goodbye.'

And he turned back towards the village.

Chapter 2

Kate O'Riordan didn't go to bars. In fact, she didn't even drink. The last time she had tasted anything alcoholic was a glass of champagne two years ago at a wedding to toast a marriage which had lasted three weeks. So what on earth was she doing in a neon-lit Manhattan bar with a cocktail in front of her?

'I think he's looking at you.'

Kate looked up at her friend Ginny, then down the bar, crowded with men in sharp suits and women in LBDs. Kate couldn't see anyone looking at her.

'Who? Where?'

'The hot blonde guy,' whispered Ginny. 'He's totally checking you out. Just act natural.'

'I am,' hissed Kate. 'This *is* me being natural.'

It was partly true, at least. Over the past few weeks, tense and anxious had begun to feel like Kate's natural state. Ginny was a good friend and had been since they had begun working at Ross Oil together, but that didn't mean Kate wanted to be set up with complete strangers, however hot they were.

As casually as she could, Kate glanced down the bar and was relieved to see the hot blonde guy air-kissing a svelte brunette.

'Ah well,' sighed Ginny, taking a sip of her drink, 'Another one bites the dust.'

Not for the first time, Kate wondered how she had allowed herself to be talked into this. It had started as a quick cocktail after work but had turned into some weird matchmaking exercise where Ginny would point out any man between eighteen and sixty, speculate on their projected income, then try to convince Kate to go and 'dazzle him' with her wit and beauty. And right now, Kate did not feel either beautiful or witty.

'Gin, I appreciate what you're trying to do, but maybe we shouldn't force this. I mean, I'm not exactly on the shelf just yet.'

Her friend took a sip of her bright pink drink and made a sympathetic face. 'Of course not. 'And you have to have time to heal, but there's always...'

'Don't say it. Please don't say it.'

'What? I was only going to say there are always plenty more fish in the sea.'

Kate let out a groan.

'There, you said it. People only say "there's plenty more fish in the sea" when you've just been dumped.'

'You haven't been dumped,' said Ginny fiercely, spilling her vodka as she sat upright. 'You're just going through a reorganisation. A restructuring.'

Ginny was in marketing at Ross Oil and she tended to use business-speak to talk about everything, but for once, Ginny had hit the nail on the head. Restructuring was how exactly how it felt. Since splitting up with her boyfriend-stroke-future-husband David, Kate had felt like everything needed to change. She'd thrown out most of her clothes, she'd bought a whole set of sheets and towels. She had even ordered a new sofa, not that she really had the room in her tiny apartment. Kate felt herself sliding into a somber mood.

'What's the point, Ginny? I mean, David was the last eligible, straight, sane man in Manhattan.'

'Not sane,' said Ginny, holding up one unsteady finger. 'Any man who will dump – excuse me, *downsize* – a woman as smart and beautiful as you has to be koo-koo,' she span her finger in a circle next to her head. 'Okay, that's making me dizzy,' she said, pushing her glass away.

'But what if he is sane?' said Kate, 'What if it was a rational decision? What if he decided I wasn't good enough?'

'Nonsense! What more could he want?'

It was fine for Ginny to say that. She was pretty, ambitious and respected. Plus she had the sort of Ivy League background employers – and the eligible bachelors of New York City – all wanted. Kate on the other hand had needed to fight every inch of the way to become head of development at Ross Oil and she was only just managing to keep her head above water in the shark tank of the boardroom. Sure, she was doing okay. Ross Oil's CEO Leo Stein liked her and she'd just nailed an offshore project in Norway. But men? There Kate was, as Ginny might say, on a downward trend. Before David, Kate hadn't managed to maintain a relationship beyond six months. Six weeks was nearer the mark, in fact. Which was why she had thought David – almost a year of dating! A near miracle! – had been The One. And David Schwartz was a catch. Handsome, smart, charming, he was also clearly going places in the corporate world. Unfortunately, David was going places in *her* corporate world: David was, technically, her boss. Which, now they were no longer an item, made things awkward to say the least.

'You don't need David, anyway, you don't need any man,' said Ginny, gesturing with her glass. 'No woman needs a man. We're career women! We make our own way in the world.'

Kate looked at her friend. She had suspected Ginny was getting drunk, but now she was now sure of it, especially as there was now more of her drink on the bar than in her glass.

'Maybe I don't need a man,' said Kate, gently taking the glass from Ginny and setting it down. 'But I'd like one to stick around for more than a few months.'

'You will! Men are...' Ginny frowned, trying to come up with the right words. '...idiots.'

'But what if they're not, Gin? I mean, David was always telling me how I needed to change my hair or read different books or...Ginny?'

Her friend was looking at her phone.

'Sorry babe,' she said, slipping off her stool and heading for the door. 'Have to take this.'

'Great,' said Kate, watching her go. 'Story of my life. Can't even hold onto my best friend.'

Leaving her glass on the bar, Kate walked through the crowded room out to the twelfth floor balcony. This was why The Summit was the hottest bar on the West Side right now: it was right in the heart of things, but it also had a view of the Hudson, shimmering with the orange lights of Jersey on the far shore. In the daytime, you'd be able to see the sludgy water and the trash barges full of squawking birds, but now? Now it was beautiful, the toxic reality hidden beneath the glistening reflections. *Fitting really*, she thought as she looked around at the drinkers, smoking and chatting and laughing. All surface, no substance.

But this is what you came here for, Katie, she thought to herself.

Everyone came to Manhattan to 'be a part of it', as the song went, to become a shiny new cog in the bustling machine, a glamorous woman in expensive heels dashing into glittering parties and drinking cocktails in rooftop bars.

Kate sighed. *Doesn't stop you feeling lonely and slightly sick twelve floors up, gazing at a filthy river*. It wasn't that Kate had failed: by any standards, she was doing well. It was more that New York hadn't given her what she'd been hoping for. And what was that? A man? Ginny was right, she didn't need a man. And she certainly didn't need David. No, the Big Apple had failed to give Kate her *ideal* man, the perfect partner she had carried around in her head since she was twelve years old. *That* was what she had come here to find. Kate prided herself on being a modern woman: she could wear Louboutins to work and still kick ass in the boardroom, but at the same time, she was also an incurable romantic and she couldn't shake the idea that there was one perfect man out there somewhere, just waiting to meet her eyes across a crowded room. Admittedly, that particular fantasy might be due to a mis-spent youth reading novels where dashing dukes fell in passionate-but-forbidden love with maids or governesses. Or perhaps it was her grandfather and his blarney. Irish born and bred, Gramps had loved to tell tall tales of Auld Ireland; rousing yarns of achingly handsome men losing their hearts to equally strong flame-haired maidens. And that was where Kate had formulated her idea of a dream man: he would be rugged and manly, with arms like gateposts, but he would also be sweet and brave and resourceful. And his green eyes would never, ever stray from Kate's. Never once.

There was a polite cough and Kate looked up. The hot blonde guy was standing next to her.

'Hey, I saw you back there at the bar,' he said. 'Can I buy you a drink?'

She looked him up and down. He was good-looking in a preppy, self-satisfied kind of way. His suit was expensive, his shoes Italian and the watch peeping out from his neatly-pressed cuff was a Breitling: New York girls could spot those sort of things in a glance. And Ginny was right, he *was* kind of hot. But she couldn't imagine him rescuing a sheep from a cliff. Or storming the ramparts of a castle. Or singing a ballad by an open fire.

'Sorry, but no,' said Kate, smiling at him as she pushed away from the balcony. 'I'm sure you are rich and connected and well on your way to being a partner in a top law firm, but you're just not what I'm looking for.'

She left the guy open-mouthed as she threaded her way through the bar and into the elevator, smiling to her reflection in the mirrored walls as she slid down towards street level. Because right then, Kate knew exactly what she was looking for. And it wasn't David, it wasn't Hot Blonde Guy and it wasn't even Manhattan. As she stepped out into the warm night, Kate saw Ginny with her cell clamped to her ear, deep in earnest conversation. She stopped abruptly when she saw Kate and covered her phone.

'What's up? Everything okay?'

'Got to go,' said Kate, blowing her a kiss, then raising an arm to flag a taxi down.

'What? Why?' said Ginny.

'Because I've got a big day tomorrow.'

The cab slid to the kerb.

'Tomorrow?' called Ginny. 'What's happening tomorrow?'

Kate opened the door and got inside.

'The beginning of the rest of my life.'

Chapter 3

Kate had planned her speech all morning. In the bathroom mirror as she'd brushed her teeth, on the subway pushed up against a fat man, in the elevator coming up to the office. First she was going to list her many attributes and achievements, but she dismissed that approach: too whiny. So she changed tack: pitch the project, sell the facts and the benefits to the company. But then he knew all that, didn't he? After all, that was one of the reasons they'd split up. So she decided to keep it simple: just tell him what she wanted. Kate strode into the office and stood in front of his desk, hands on hips.

'David, I want the Irish project.'

David looked up at her, blinking in surprise. Perhaps she should have opened with 'good morning' or 'nice tie'. David hated pushy women. He'd never said as much – that wouldn't go down well in the modern touchy-feely corporate environment – but Kate knew David. He didn't even like waitresses suggesting the specials.

Collecting himself, David nodded and steepled his

fingers in front of his lips. Even when they'd been dating, Kate had hated the smug way David sat behind his desk. Like a king. She stared at him willing him to say something, to react, even if it was to laugh.

'Okay,' he said.

'Okay?'

He nodded again. 'Sure, why not?'

Kate narrowed her eyes. Was this a trick?

'Actually I was just discussing this with Leo,' said David, 'He agrees that Ireland is a strong opportunity. He gave me the green light.'

Leo gave *him* the go-ahead? Kate bit her tongue, refraining from reminding him that had been her project from the start. But then he knew that too, didn't he? He knew Kate had done all the work on the Ireland eco project in her spare time: two months crunching the numbers and looking at the data, three months poring over geological surveys, ocean charts and meteorological records, plus another month or so to put together the budget. But that was when Kate had made her big mistake. She had casually mentioned what she had been working on to David over dinner one night. He had nodded and yawned. 'Send me the files,' he said, 'I'll look it over.'

By the Monday of the next week, Ireland was David's project. At their morning conference meeting, Leo Gough their CEO had announced that David would be heading up the development of 'an exciting left-field project in Ireland', praising David for his 'vision' and 'daring'.

Kate had managed not to scream in the boardroom. Just. She had waited until she and David were alone in his office – right where she was standing now, in fact, before she had unleashed her tirade. He was a snake, a coward and a thief, she had said. He couldn't spell integrity, much less show any. David had shrugged and countered that he was doing her a favor: Leo would never have trusted someone 'of your experience' with such a big project. Kate was not proud of her response to that. Either way, the ensuing row had been the beginning of the end for Kate and David. Who could stay with someone who put his ambition over their relationship? She had demanded he hand back the key to her apartment and it wasn't until then that Kate had realized that David had never given her a key to his place. She would have loved to have thrown it at him. She would have liked to have walked out on the job too, but she had far too much invested in it.

'Of course, I will be running the operation,' said David. 'But you will be my eyes and ears on the ground.'

Ah. Now it made sense. He wanted her expertise, but also wanted her out of the office. That way he could claim all the credit if it was a success. And distance himself from the mess if it wasn't.

'Well thank you so much for the opportunity,' said Kate. 'I'm so pleased you thought of me.' Her sarcasm went over his head. He leant back in his chair and spread his hands.

'Who else, baby?'

'Don't baby me, Mr. Schwartz,' she said. 'I don't think it's appropriate.'

He glanced towards the door, checking it was closed.

'Kate, come on,' he said, lowering his voice. 'We don't need to make this personal, do we?'

'Absolutely not. Professional all the way.'

She raised her head with what she hoped looked like dignity. 'When do you want me to leave?'

'Oh, straight away. And Kate? This is a big opportunity – for both of us. I don't need to tell you how much the company needs a win in this area, do I? If you can sell this to the people over there, it's going to look real nice on your resume.'

'Oh I have no intention of needing a resume,' said Kate, turning on her heel. 'You, however, might want to think about refreshing yours.'

Chapter 4

Connor raised his hands to the baying crowd.

'Now then, keep it down,' he shouted. 'One at a time.'

It felt as though most of the village was crammed into the bar of the pub. Not that this was particularly unusual; Connor's was the hub of Clover Cove. If the pub was open, it was full of faces and noise. A meeting place, dance hall and a shelter from the elements, both meteorological and emotional, the pub was the rock beneath the community. Connor's father Cormac had run the place, and his grandfather before; the pub had history, it had weight. Which was why so many elbows were leant on the scarred oak bar, red faces shouting the odds. They came here for weddings, funerals and festivals. And they came for reassurance.

'What if they knock down the church?' asked Mikey the blacksmith.

'What if they knock down the *pub*?' shouted Kenneth the butcher.

Connor clapped his hands.

'Alright, alright. Let's not get carried away. Remember the Ross Oil thing is just a rumor at the moment.'

'Oh no, Dick Doyle heard it from Mary,' said Raff the fisherman. 'And she heard it from her cousin Susanne. You know, the one who works in Ballymain?'

'Susanne at the telephone exchange?' said Orla from the Post Office.

There was a gasp. Susanne at the telephone exchange was regarded locally as the equivalent of the Oracle of Delphi.

'And Danny Brennan's writing about it in the Examiner, so it must be true,' added Raff.

'Raff, you spoke to Danny,' said Connor. 'What did he say?'

The big man ran a thoughtful hand over his stubble.

'Apparently, the Ross Oil people are being very tight-lipped, wouldn't say they were going to build in the Cove, but they didn't say they weren't either.'

Connor nodded. It wasn't the first time the oil industry had shown interest in the village. Back in the '90s, when the fishing in Clover Cove was dying out, there had been plans to run a pipeline from the oil rigs out in the Atlantic, or even to rebuild the harbor as a docking point for tankers. Clover Cove was by this point already a forgotten backwater, but it had one of the few deep ports on the west coast, which made it valuable. Or vulnerable, depending on your point of view.

'Well, I say we take the money.'

Connor looked up sharply as a handsome young man walked through the door. *Ryan.* Of course it was Ryan. Six years apart, they had the same DNA and they both supported the local hurling team, but beyond that, Connor and Ryan couldn't be more different. Connor was solid, reliable, while Ryan was impulsive and wild. No great wonder that they seemed to clash over everything.

'You remember what happened the last time these oil

people came for us, Con,' said Ryan. 'Our father was the first to man the barricades. But times have changed.'

Connor looked at his little brother, feeling annoyance and, yes, a little grudging pride. Ryan could be headstrong and irritating, but sometimes it was like looking into a mirror. Not only because Ryan had the same dark hair and green eyes – all the James kids had inherited their mother's good looks – but because ten years ago, that would have been him, striding through the village, calling for change, passionate and obstinate.

'Our Da passed on, Ryan,' said Connor. 'And you're right times have changed, but...'

'They've not changed fast enough, brother.'

Connor threw a hard look towards his younger sibling. The last thing he needed right now was one of Ryan's 'power to the people' rants, but Ryan ignored the warning.

'Clover Cove is dying here, Con. We've no doctor, no school, no new jobs. What's attracting new families to move here?'

'Beautiful country, a sense of community...'

'Sure, and can't they get that anywhere on the West Coast? Why *here*, Connor? Don't you think we need more investment? The oil people will give us that.'

'Heaven knows we could do with the money,' said Molly from the cafe. 'The potholes on the Wenn road are big enough to swallow a cow.'

'Sure, and that's true, Mol,' nodded Connor. 'But we have to balance the benefits of the money with everything we'd lose.'

'What have we got to lose?' shouted Mikey from the back. 'Our jewels?'

There were a few weak laughs, but Connor didn't smile.

'We have a great deal to lose, Michael. A great deal. Yes, I know it doesn't always feel like much, but we have a real community here. Families who have been here generations. Families who stick together through the hard times.'

'Like ours you mean?'

Connor glared at his brother. It was a low blow. Since the death of their father and their mother's disappearance abroad, Connor and Ryan were all that were left of the once-mighty James clan. Brother Luke had joined the navy, sister Marion had moved to Boston. The Jameses flown to the winds, living new lives.

'It's true we've lost a few over the years,' said Connor, addressing the whole bar. 'But all the more reason we have to pull together on this.' He glanced across at Ryan. 'And I'm not saying we should say jump one way or the other. Maybe Ryan's right, maybe it is time to change. I'm just saying let's be calm about this. Think it through.'

There was a pause, then everyone was shouting at once. *Calm.* It was like asking a flock of gulls to be calm when Raff threw bait off the back of his boat. Money was money and Connor knew he couldn't expect sober reflection when a giant American oil company was dangling endless riches above their heads. His Da had loved that Otis Redding song 'You Don't Miss Your Water', and was always punching it up on the jukebox. *You don't miss your water*, Otis used to sing, *until your well runs dry.* They were too giddy, too excited by the possibilities to see that what they had here was worth holding onto. And how easily it could slip away.

'So how much does a Jacuzzi cost anyway?' called Mikey above the hullaballoo.

Everyone laughed. Everyone except Connor.

Chapter 5

Ireland was green, that much was true. Kate looked out of the window of the bus, open-mouthed. The fields on either side were a dark emerald, the hedges and the sycamores were green too, each a different variation on the next, each scattered with tiny glistening raindrops from the last cloud burst. Which, Kate supposed, was the reason it was so green. But when the sun shone, *oh my*. It was everything she had imagined and more. Twisting lanes, edged by stone walls and wound by ivy, shining pools and little hilltop copses of oak. Sudden villages painted pastel pink, clipped churchyards and cozy pubs. She expected Maureen O'Hara to come striding across the meadow at any moment. And being raised high up at the back of the bus, she could drink it all in, like a private audience with Ireland.

Kate actually couldn't remember the last time she had been on a bus. Living in New York, it wasn't really necessary: you used the subway if you were going top to bottom or cabs if you were going side to side. Manhattan traffic was too congested for buses, but out here in Ireland, the bus was the only choice, it seemed. Kate had flown from JFK to

Dublin, then caught a half-empty prop-plane into tiny Knock airport, which had only one cab company – and, according to the lady at the counter, only one driver, who was 'sleeping it off'. So the bus was the only option if you wanted to head west and Kate had been the only passenger when it set off from the airport, slowly picking up passengers as they edged their way into the green embrace of the Irish countryside, the rain coming again, washing down the glass.

'Looks like a black one,' said the woman next to her. She was fiftyish with a headscarf and a blue waxed jacket; she had joined the bus at a village called Downalaing.

'A black one?' asked Kate.

'The clouds, doesn't look like they're for shifting. The rain's in for the day.'

Kate craned her neck; all she could see now was grey sky and she wasn't even sure what that meant. That was another funny thing about Manhattan; you never looked up. Even if you had been looking out for clues about the rain – and wasn't that what the Weather Channel was for? – it was hard to actually see much beyond the towering skyscrapers. Living in NYC was like living at the bottom of a well.

'American, is it?' Asked a red-faced man in a flat cap.

'Yes, from New York actually.'

'Ah, old Gotham City,' said the man wistfully. 'I used to love *Batman* when I was a lad.'

Kate couldn't imagine the man as a child. He looked like he'd been carved from a log.

'You visiting relatives, darling?'

Another woman had joined in. Clearly the opening about the weather was just a formality. Kate saw that everyone on the bus was looking at her expectantly. She supposed she was an oddity with her big silver suitcase and impractical shoes.

'Relatives? No, not really. I'm here for work actually. Although I'm told I do have family around here. Or rather, my grandfather did. O'Riordan,' said Kate. 'That's my grandfather's name. Mine too.'

Kate felt a sudden upsurge in interest: not only were the passengers listening, they were all sitting forward, not wanting to miss a word. She smiled, remembering her grandfather's tall tales about 'the old country', the warmth of the locals, the tight knit community where everyone knew each other's business and everything could be settled over a pint.

'O'Riordan you say?' asked the man, 'Would he be one of the Ballymanor O'Riordans?'

'No,' said Kate, 'I don't think so. Or at least, he didn't mention Ballymanor. Is that near here?'

The woman lent forward, frowning. 'Not the Tormary O'Riordans?'

Kate shook her head. smiling nervously, wondering whether it was a good or a bad thing Gramps hadn't come from Tormary, wherever that was.

'No, he was from Glendoogan, not too far from Clover Cove.'

Kate saw the woman's eyes widen.

'The Glendoogan O'Riordans,' she said to the bus, to audible gasps. Kate looked around anxiously.

'Is there a problem?'

The woman inched away from her, clutching her shopping bag tighter.

'Now then Mary,' said the ruddy-faced man. 'Give the girl a chance. What did you say was your granddaddy's name?'

'Gerry. Gerry O'Riordan.'

'Gerry O'Riordan, you say,' said the old man, looking up at the ceiling. 'Gerry, Gerry, Gerry. Was it the Gerry who had the horse?'

'No Patrick, this girl's talking about the Gerry who broke the pipe.'

'The pipe?' said the man, looking sharply at Kate. '89 that was, the year of the storm.'

'Gar'cher, the storm was in '91. And the Gerry who broke the pipe would have been a grown man by then.'

'Your grandfather, hen,' said the first lady. 'Was he a tall man?'

'Fairly tall, yes.'

'Not him then,' she said with satisfaction.

'And did he wear a hat?' asked the man.

'I couldn't say. I've only known him when he was living in America.'

'The Gerry with the hat is still living with his sister out at Abbey Island, you old fool.'

'His father was a vet, a veterinarian, I can tell you that.'

There was a loud exhalation throughout the bus.

'Gerry O'Riordan, the vet's son? The Gerry who burnt the stable down?' She leant forward and took Kate's hand in hers. 'I'm so sorry.'

'Why? What happened?'

The woman pursed her lips and gave a small shake of the head.

'It's not for me to say. Besides, you seem like a lovely young girl.'

Kate suddenly jerked forward as the bus pulled up. They were in a square, a simple stone church set back behind a raised wall.

'Clover Cove!' bellowed the driver. 'Clover COVE!'

'Oh, that's me,' said Kate, getting up so fast she banged her head on the roof.

'Hmmf. Just like her granddaddy,' said the old man.

Staggering her way down the aisle, dragging her shiny suitcase, Kate noted that the rest of the passengers had turned away from her, suddenly very interested in something outside the bus. She couldn't understand it. Perhaps they had mistaken what she had said.

'Thank you,' she said to the driver, but he just harrumphed and pulled a lever for the door.

'Oh. Well, goodbye all.'

She stepped down onto the wet roadway, immediately feeling the rain against her neck and shoulders. She flipped up the collar of her trench coat and waved as the bus moved away, spraying her with water. Wishing for an umbrella, she pulled out the case's handle and sized up her surroundings.

Apart from the soft hiss of the rain, all was quiet: the square was completely deserted, not even a parked car.

'Welcome to Ireland,' she muttered, stepping into a puddle.

Okay, let's get moving, she thought decisively. Ireland might be small and, well, less developed than New York, but it was still an important territory. She needed this to work and standing around in the rain wasn't getting her anywhere. Kate looked around. With the church to her right, there was a short line of stores straight ahead.

Coffee. The word leapt into her head. It was the one thing guaranteed to make her feel human after a long flight. Plus it might warm her up, she thought, hunching her shoulders. Kate waddled across the puddle-pocked tarmac, trying not to look down at her suede heels; they were certain to be ruined and she doubted there was anywhere she could replace them within a day's travel. She pushed the door of what looked like a grocery store. It didn't move. 'Closed' read the sign in the window. Kate stepped back. The same sign in every window: all the stores were closed.

Odd: it was mid-afternoon. Where *was* everybody?

She dragged the suitcase back across the square towards a large blue building she assumed was the pub. 'Connor's', read the sign, with smaller letters in gold which Kate assumed was Gaelic: 'Go n-éirí an bóthar leat'.

It looked like some sort of greeting, but it made Kate feel even more uncomfortable. She realized she had no idea of the customs of this place: could an unaccompanied woman walk into a pub? Did you need to use a special entrance? It sounded crazy, but she didn't want to make a mis-step, didn't want to alienate the populace any further on her first day. As she wavered by the door, the cry of a seagull reminded her that she was near the sea.

Well, might as well get the lay of the land, she thought, heading down a steep lane: she could see nothing beyond the drizzle, but downhill had to be the way to the sea. The lane twisted back and forth, cottages on either side, no sign of life anywhere, increasing Kate's feeling of isolation. On the bus, they had talked of horses and hats and mentioned tongue-twisting place names, each of them connected to this wet land by family and tradition and endless bus rides. Everyone in Ireland seemed to know who they were and where they came from; Kate certainly couldn't say the same, especially so far from New York. Here, she was a rootless foreigner, no family to speak of, no friends and a job she was barely clinging to. She had come here hoping to feel some spark of recognition deep inside her, but it just looked grey and depressing.

'And where's the ocean gone?' she said, stopping at the end of the path. Not only had the people disappeared, so had the sea. Kate could sense it was out there somewhere, but it was like standing inside a grey cloud. She could barely see three steps in front of her, let alone the water. It was then she heard the music. Pop music, not fiddly-diddly Irish music. The kind of music you'd hear coming from a boutique in Soho or the Village. Kate turned towards it, not really knowing where she was going, just following the breadcrumbs, trusting them to lead her out of the forest. And there it was. A small cottage facing – she guessed – the beach, a sign made from shells reading 'Molly's Cafe'. Pop music and coffee! Eagerly, Kate pushed the door and it opened with the friendly tinkle.

She shook her coat and looked around. Mismatched chairs and tables, each with a little flower display, cupcake pink walls and a clock made from a dancing cat. Kate immediately felt at home, especially when the smell of freshly-brewed coffee reached her nose. As she stepped towards the counter, a pretty dark-haired woman appeared, wiping her hands on an apron.

'Sorry, you caught me doing the washing up.' The woman seemed to give her a double-take.

'Oh, I thought you were Mary from the farm. You're not, are you?'

Kate smiled.

'No, not Mary from the farm. I'm Kate O'Riordan from, well, the States.'

The woman's eyes opened wide. 'The *United* States? Well it's been a long time since we had any visitors from so far away. And look at the welcome we're giving you – you're soaked!'

Kate glanced at her shoulders. Her cotton trench coat was indeed wet through. Clearly the Irish tourist board had picked sunny days when they were taking their publicity photographs.

'Didn't really pack for the weather I'm afraid,' said Kate.

'I can see. Here,' said the woman, leaning across to hand Kate a garish towel. 'We're used to this, even if you aren't.'

Kate dabbed at her face and her hair. It felt like she'd been through a car wash.

'Well, I'm Molly and this is my cafe,' said the girl. 'We also double as the bakery and sometimes the fishmongers. Everything you need is here and a lot more besides you don't.'

She pointed to an inflatable flamingo, which looked slightly saggy.

'Got that for the tourists, but there's not much call since they built the bypass. All the visitors go to Balligan Rocks now and not many of them at this time of year.'

She fixed Kate with a shrewd look.

'So what brings you to Clover Cove, Kate O'Riordan?'

'Business. I'm with Ross Oil.'

Kate had expected a nonplussed shrug, but the woman simply nodded.

'So you'll be the one wanting to buy my cafe, will you?'

Kate felt her mouth open and close, before stuttering, 'No, we're just looking into the possibility of siting a development nearby. How... how did you know about it?'

Molly leant across the counter and passed her a newspaper.

The Kilmara Examiner read the masthead above a splash headline:

'Oil Giant To Tear Coast Apart'.

Kate put a hand over her mouth as she scanned the story.

'Exclusive by Daniel T. Brennan, chief reporter. Leaked reports suggest multinational conglomerate Ross Oil is to pump billions into Kiln County. Ross PR refused to comment on the nature of the project, but did not deny a substantial investment was imminent. Local experts

speculate on a pipeline landfall or processing plant for the drilling platforms in the Hanover oil field west of Blackshod Head. Locals have reacted with fury to the news, with one landowner vowing to 'fight these Yanks tooth and nail', while councillors have expressed 'deep concern' over potential damage to the environment and the 'legendary beauty of our coastline'.

'Oh no,' whispered Kate, her eyes darting back to the phrase 'leaked reports'. Leaked? Who would do such a thing? David? Her heart dropped. *Of course* it was David. It was exactly the sort of thing he'd do and it would be much simpler for him if Kate failed. Out of the office was good, but out of the company was even better.

'Ach, I shouldn't take it to heart,' said Molly kindly, 'That Dan Brennan at the paper's always trying to stir things up. Bad news is good news for the local rag.'

Kate forced a smile.

'Well, I suppose it saves me explaining why I'm here.'

'Oh, it's all anyone's been talking about for the past week.'

'A week?' said Kate, looking at the woman, then back at the date on the paper. 'You've known about it for a *week*? I didn't even know I was coming two days ago.'

Woman smiled.

'Suzanne at the telephone exchange had it from her cousin Gregory whose brother Cian works on the rigs; a diver I think. All the Ross Oil workers have been talking about something happening in the Cove.'

Kate closed her eyes. Of course. She had asked for surveys from the rigs during her research; she should have known it would trigger this kind of speculation.

'Nothing much happens around here we don't hear

about before it's in the news,' said Molly. 'The mobile phone is patchy, but we're not entirely isolated you know.'

Kate nodded, trying to keep the dismay from her face. Fumbling with the unfamiliar money in her purse, she pulled out a note to pay for the paper.

'Ach, you can keep it,' said Molly. 'Something to put in your report, I suppose. So you'll be staying at the pub?'

Kate pulled a damp piece of paper from her open purse. 'The Clover Cove Suites and Spa', she read. 'Could you direct me?'

'Oh, it's straight back up to the square. Big blue building, can't miss it.'

Kate frowned.

'Isn't that the pub?'

'Aye. Pub, hotel, meeting room and confessional if you listen to some of the old boys sitting at the bar.'

'And it's a... spa?'

Siobhan laughed. 'Welcome to Ireland. We like to spin a yarn.'

Kate turned to go.

'Sure I'll be seeing you again Kate O'Riordan,' said Molly. 'Give me a good price for the cafe now and you'll be getting a discount on your croissants.'

'You do croissants?'

Molly cocked a thumb toward her chest.

'Cordon Bleu trained. Bake them fresh every morning, bread too. All yours for the right price.'

'Seriously, whatever the newspaper says, I'm only here to take a few photos and consider the possibilities.'

'Uh-huh,' said Molly, nodding sceptically. 'I'll be waiting.'

Chapter 6

'It's not "play it again Sam," said Raff the fisherman, 'It's "play it, Sam."'

'No,' said Alan the postman, 'Bogart says "Play it again Sam." Everyone knows that.'

Connor looked at the men and tried his best not to react. He lifted the glass he was polishing up to the light, squinting.

'Actually, boys,' he said, 'Bogart just says "play it," he doesn't use the fella's name at all.'

'Is that so?' said Raff.

'It is,' said Connor. And it wasn't the first time he'd had to settle this particular argument either. When they'd had a few drinks, the patrons of the bar often got themselves into discussions about movies, despite there not having been a cinema within an hour's drive of Clover Cove since the 1970s. Which was why they were arguing about *Casablanca*, he supposed.

'Of all the gin joints in all the towns in all the world,' he quoted, 'She walks into...'

Connor's Bogart impression was interrupted as the

saloon door banged open and a woman ran into the bar. Her hair was wet from the rain and she was still pulling her arm into her coat.

'She's here!'

Alan swivelled on his seat.

'Lord love you, Kitty Doyle,' he said, 'What are you doing rushing about like that?'

'Quiet, you old fool,' she snapped, 'This is serious. It's the woman from Ross Oil: she's here!'

That brought a shocked silence to the bar for two seconds, then everyone started talking at once.

'Alright, alright,' said Connor, stepping out from behind the bar, patting the air with both hands. 'Everyone hush a while.' He stepped across to the woman. 'Now then, Kitty, have you actually seen this lady?'

Kitty shook her head.

'Pat Mooney was on the bus, Con. He spoke to the girl. She's American, got a huge silver suitcase.'

'And do we know for sure she's with the oil company?'

'Well, she said she was here to work. What else was she going to do?'

'She could be one of those vloggers,' said Raff.

'Or a rapper,' said Mikey.

Kitty rolled her eyes and turned back to Connor.

'Her name's O'Riordan. Kate O'Riordan.'

This bought a gasp from the bar.

'The Ballymanor O'Riordans?'

Connor held up both hands. The last thing he wanted was to get into all that.

'And where is she now?'

'No one knows. Pat said she got off in the square; then he called me and I came straight down. She wasn't out there when I came across, that's for sure.'

‘Do you think she’s gone up to the Castle?’ asked Orla from the post office.

Connor crossed to the window and peered up at the skies. ‘Looks like a storm for sure.’

‘Coming down cats and dogs already,’ agreed Kitty, shaking her collar for good measure. Connor clucked his tongue. If the woman tried to walk anywhere, let alone taking the cliff path, she was likely to slip onto the rocks.

‘Raff, take the controls,’ said Connor. ‘I’m going to find her.’

Chapter 7

The rain seemed to have increased and Kate quickened her pace to trot as she crossed the square, her suitcase bucking over the wet tarmac. How *had* the leak happened? It was true that Ross Oil's interest in the village had to come out sometime, but even so, it certainly made her job all the harder. She had wanted to speak quietly to the local landowners and influential people, persuade them the Ross plan was in their interest and get them on-side before it became public knowledge. Obviously now people were going to jump to conclusions and panic. In fact, they clearly already had.

'*Oil Giant To Tear Coast Apart*' indeed. Kate supposed she could hardly blame the paper for such sensationalism. After all, the Petro-Chemical industry hadn't exactly been dynamite at considering people's feelings in the past.

Kate paused at the door of the pub. She could smell the hops and hear music inside. Irish music this time. Swallowing, she put one hand on the door handle, picturing the stranger entering the saloon in all those old cowboy movies, where the piano player stops and everyone turns to stare.

Come on Kate, you're a kick-ass business woman, she scolded herself. She had walked into boardrooms and faced down some of the most fearsome CEOs in the corporate world, it was ridiculous to be intimidated by a few old Irish men.

'Be brave,' she whispered, stepping forward purposefully – just as the door whipped open. Kate stumbled forward, one ankle turning, hands clutching at the air and fell headlong – into the arms of a man. Wavy dark hair drooping over his creased brow, high cheekbones and the greenest eyes she had ever seen. He was handsome, that much she grasped immediately. But he was scowling down at her.

'D'you make a habit of falling into bars, d'ya?' he growled, lifting Kate upright.

'So sorry,' blustered Kate, 'I was just pushing the door, I didn't know you were behind it.'

'Obviously,' he muttered.

Embarrassed, Kate tried to pull herself up straight and promptly tripped over her suitcase.

'Oh no,' she gasped.

'Well, you're welcome,' glowered the man and turned on his heel.

'Yes, thank you,' she called after him, her cheeks flaring. 'Thank you for, well, catching me.'

The dark-haired man shrugged his broad shoulders and flicked a hand dismissively in Kate's direction. *Well, that was rude,* she thought, her anger rising. She was just about to say something when she became aware of a man standing by her elbow.

'Miss O'Riordan, is it?' he said with a wide grin, thrusting a pink hand in her direction. The man was thirty-ish, with a round weather-beaten face, his red cheeks glowing from beneath a scuff of beard. If Hollywood had been casting 'Rugged Irish Fisherman,' they would need look no further; every box was ticked, even down to the captain's hat and vague smell of the sea.

'Yes, yes, I'm Kate O'Riordan,' Kate stammered, shaking his proffered hand.

'Geoff Rafferty, pleased to make your acquaintance,' he said, 'Now will you come in and have a drink?'

'Yes, thank you – but how did you know my name?'

'Ach, nothing much happens in the Cove without it making social media,' said the fisherman and a lean man in gumboots sitting at the bar held up his cell phone and waggled it by way of illustration. 'It's all over Twitter already. That's why Connor was behind the door there – he was coming to find you. We were worried you'd got lost.'

'Oh, that's very kind,' said Kate vaguely towards the dark-haired man who was now sitting at the end of the bar, but he merely gave another half-shrug.

'Now then,' said Raff the fisherman taking her arm. 'Let's get you introduced, shall we?'

He gently steered her around the pub, introducing her to the various people sitting at tables by the open fire and by the bar. 'This is Orla, she's the post-mistress. That's Billy, he's the butcher. Was, anyway, when we had a butcher. And this is Mikey, he's the local eejit.'

The bar erupted into laughter and Kate was glad that her awkward entrance had been forgotten; people actually seemed interested to meet her. She allowed herself to be introduced to a bewildering range of Daveys, Liams and at least three Marys. She quickly realized that this was why the village was deserted: everyone was in the bar.

'Now, what can I get you?' asked the fisherman when they finally circled back to the bar. 'You're looking a tad drenched there, Miss Katherine, I'd go for a hot toddy.'

'Kettle's broke,' said the dark-haired man.

'Well then, how about a pint of the black stuff?'

'Black?' said Kate.

Geoff laughed. 'Guinness, girl. The Irish national drink.'

'Oh I'm afraid I don't really drink,' she said, trying not to think of that night in The Summit and the hot blonde guy.

'Ah now, the Guinness isn't really drink,' said the thin man with the cell phone. 'Your Guinness is more like a medicine, a tonic to keep off the chill when you've been in the rain.'

Kate began to demur, but Geoff held up a hand.

'Euan was the chemist over in Port Quinn, before it closed,' he said with a sly smile. 'You can't deny a medical man's opinion, can you? It's practically a prescription.'

Kate looked up in the green eyes of the dark-haired man – Connor, was it? – and saw the distain. Just some stupid American coming over here with her suitcase of cash. But Kate reminded herself she needed to keep these people onside. Plus she was annoyed at the way Connor was looking at her.

'Sure, I'll have one,' she said, sticking her chin out a little. She didn't want him to think she was a prude. 'Why not?'

'Grand,' said Geoff. 'Connor, if you'd do the honors?'

Slowly, reluctantly, the dark-haired man slid down from his stool and walked behind the bar, selecting a glass from a shelf and spinning it casually in his hand. *Of course,* thought Kate, the penny finally dropping. The pub was called 'Connor's'. He was the landlord.

'Sorry, you're Connor James?' said Kate, 'Manager of the hotel and spa? I didn't realize. I'm Kate O'Riordan, I think we exchanged emails.' She pulled out the damp paper she had shown to Molly in the cafe. 'I have a deluxe suite booked in the Suites and Spa?'

Connor nodded slowly as he concentrated on pouring the Guinness. 'So you do,' he said.

Kate frowned and looked around the room. 'Is it nearby? The hotel I mean?'

'Oh yes, very close,' said Connor, placing a glass of thick black beer on the counter. 'In fact it's about four feet above your head.'

There was laughter as Kate looked up, seeing a black rough-hewn wooden beam and a sagging yellow roof. 'That's... the spa?' she said, her hopes of a Shiatsu massage rapidly fading.

'Well now, it does have a spa bath,' he said. Pausing for dramatic effect, he added, 'although it doesn't exactly work at the moment. Your man Raff here has been promising to fix it for months.'

'Now I was going to get around to that,' he said. 'It's just the parts are having to come from Sweden. Isn't the EU a grand thing?'

Kate took a dainty sip of beer and tried not to wrinkle her nose. She was aware that most of the eyes in the room were on her and she didn't want to make matters any worse than they already were.

'That's delicious,' she said, taking another, larger pull and looking at Euan the chemist. 'Is it really good for you? I remember my Grandfather saying something to that effect.'

'Ah, well I'm not sure Bishop Ray would agree with me,' said Euan, 'But I'm of the opinion that a little of what you fancy does you good. In moderation, of course.'

'And what is it you fancy, Miss O'Riordan?' said Connor, his dark eyes boring into hers. *You,* she thought, angrily pushing the idea from her mind the moment it occurred. Connor James might have movie star good-looks – or he would have if he ever stopped scowling – but he was rude and unfriendly. Not her sort of man at all. *At all.*

'Fancy?' she said, flustered. 'I don't really...'

'I mean what are you here for?' He gestured to the bar. 'I think everyone would like to know what it is you're after. Is it the village you're wanting? Have you come here with your American dollars thinking you can buy anything you please?'

Kate looked around at the faces gazing at her expectantly. She had the unsettling idea that they had all been talking about her before she had walked into the bar. In fact, she had the feeling they had been preparing for her arrival for weeks.

'Now then, now then Connor,' said Raff quickly, holding up his hands. 'The poor girl's only just flown in. I'm sure she'll let us all know her plans when she's ready, but right now she'd probably like to freshen up a little, hmm?'

Raff gently took Kate's suitcase and led her towards a door next to the bar. 'If you'd like to step this way Miss, I'll show you to your room.'

As the door closed, there was a second's pause, then Kate heard the bar erupt into animated conversation. She let out a long breath. Nothing like making an entrance, was there?

'You'll have to excuse Connor, Miss Kate,' said Raff kindly, ushering her towards a flight of stairs. 'He's a grand boy when he warms up. And like all of us, he's a little... shall we say, apprehensive about the future.'

'I assure you I'm not here to harm the village, Mr. Rafferty,' said Kate.

'Oh, I can see that. But it's all people have been talking about since that thing in the *Examiner*, you can understand they're worried.'

Kate nodded and followed the fisherman into her room. It was surprisingly cozy with a large bed and a tiled fireplace with crackling logs already glowing in the hearth. Someone had certainly been expecting her.

'Thank you, Mr. Rafferty,' said Kate.

'Call me Raff, everyone does. And don't worry, worse things happen at sea.'

When he had gone, Kate sat down on the bed and stared at her suitcase, wondering whether she should even bother unpacking. It seemed as though everyone had already made up their mind about her and Ross Oil, without ever having heard the first thing about what their plans were. They could have been planning to build a giant crystal palace for all the villagers knew. Although she wasn't sure that would meet with Connor James' approval either. She curled her fingers into a fist and tried not to spit out an insult in the general direction of the man.

'Come on Kate, don't let him get to you,' she whispered.

After all, this wasn't Kate's first time at the rodeo. As Head of Development, it was her job to research possible sites for Ross Oil projects, then after board approval, she would go out to the location to see if it was feasible to pursue the idea. So she had met with hostile villagers plenty of times before, but they usually came to see that change was a positive, from a financial point of view if nothing else. Kate wasn't so sure about Clover Cove. She hadn't been here very long, but it didn't look like change was a big thing here.

She stood and walked to the window. The rain seemed to have got harder, running down the pane in ribbons, the old sash frame rattling against the wood. The lady on the bus had been right, it was 'a black one'. If Kate had believed in omens, this didn't look good.

Kate walked through to the tiny bathroom and looked hopefully at the so-called spa bath. It was an old clawfoot tub which barely looked big enough to rinse a terrier, even if the Jacuzzi feature had been working. Leaning over, she turned on the water. A disturbing clanking sound immediately came from the wall, an erratic gush of water pulsing out in time with the noise. Kate quickly turned it off. It wasn't worth flooding the lower floors for the sake of a tepid bath.

So this was her glamorous new job, she thought disconsolately, sitting on the edge of the bath. This was the reason she had gambled her career and flown thousands of miles to what felt like the other side of the world. She caught her reflection in the bathroom mirror. The rain-straggled hair, the smudged make-up and most of all, the hangdog, defeated expression. And she had only been in Ireland less than a day.

Kate closed her eyes tight, trying not to picture David's smug face as he walked into Leo's office to report Kate's failure over the Irish project. Now she could see why he had been so magnanimous about 'allowing' Kate to take the lead on this one. He couldn't really fail, could he? If it was a success, he took the credit. If it was a washout, he got rid of a rival. A win-win, as Ginny would say.

Thinking of her friend, Kate grabbed her cellphone, desperate to hear a friendly voice. She only had one bar of reception – and Kate counted herself lucky to get that. 'Here goes nothing,' she muttered, scrolling up Ginny's number and pressing 'call'.

'Hello?'

There was a hum, then a crackle and a fizzing robot voice came through.

'Ginny? Is that you?'

Silence, then suddenly her friend was speaking. '...knew it would be you, how is Ireland? I'm so jealous you get to go to all those exotic places.'

You wouldn't if you could see me now, thought Kate.

'How is it?'

'It's very... green,' she said.

'Oh I'll bet! So pretty,' enthused her friend. 'And how are the men? All cheekbones and floppy hair?'

Kate gave an ironic smile, thinking of Connor James. 'Some,' she said. 'Where are you?'

In the background, Kate could hear music and the rumble of conversation. It sounded like a pretty good party.

'What? Sorry babe,' said Ginny, raising her voice, 'You're breaking up. Listen, I'm dying to hear all about the hot farm boys, so I'll call you tonight?'

'Yes hon, *please* call,' said Kate, 'I miss you,' but she was talking to a dead line.

She looked at the screen. 'No bars. Great.'

There was a creak outside the door and Kate turned, listening. Then there was a swell of laughter from the bar. Just the old pub moving in the wind, she thought. She was going to have to get used to that, she supposed.

Sighing, Kate took off her damp jacket and lay down on the bed, wincing as it groaned under her weight. She heard raised voices, then a burst of singing from the bar below. A deep baritone: some sort of sea shanty? Seemed as though everyone was having a good time except her tonight. Her grandfather had loved the old Irish songs, making her listen to crackly old recordings on his little radiogram. *Come on Kate, don't give in to it,* she scolded herself. *You are a kick-ass New York businesswoman, you can handle anything. You will show them all.*

And just then, the light bulb in her bedside lamp gave a 'ping' and blinked out, plunging the room into darkness.

Chapter 8

Connor pushed through the door marked 'private', walking from the hubbub of the bar into the relative calm of the pub's kitchen. He leant against a pillar and banged his forehead against it. *Stupid, so stupid,* he thought. There was no call to go snapping at that poor girl from the oil company, after all. Kate, that was her name: Kate with the blue eyes and the pretty face and the...

He shook his head, forced himself to focus. Kate O'Riordan was the enemy after all. Even if she was just here to do a job. Connor assumed that was true and that she wasn't trying to destroy the community just for fun. And yet, Connor feared that it might come to that. Ever since Kate O'Riordan had left the bar, the old debate had been raging back and forth again, the pros and cons of Ross Oil coming to Clover Cove. The pros: the money, of course. Mikey was going to get a speedboat, Aiden was going to buy his Auntie Jean a house 'with those stone lions by the door' and everyone else was going to go on exotic holidays, although he seriously doubted any of them would get any further than Dublin.

Only one voice was advising caution: his. Connor James, the only man who seemed to care about the Cove. The irony was almost overwhelming. And by the looks he was getting back – the hurt, sulky looks of children who'd had their toys taken away on Christmas morning – he knew he was unlikely to get much support – not right now anyway. They were too excited, too dazzled by the imaginary checks to see the danger to this close little community they all took for granted. Money equalled greed equalled villagers falling over each other to sell up, leaving Clove Cove a ghost town. Buildings would be gone, people gone too, off on their world cruises or isolated in their mansions with only stone lions for company, replaced by itinerant workers from across the globe until the work was done. And then? Well, what then? Another chunk of Ireland gone to foreign money, another few miles of pristine coast lost. And who would miss it?

'Me, I'll miss it,' he whispered to no-one in particular.

'Talkin' to yerself again, Con?'

He turned and not for the first time was struck with the odd sensation of seeing himself in reflection.

'Ryan,' he said, letting out a sigh. Connor supposed there was a certain kind of ego involved in thinking his younger brother resembled him so closely. Ryan James was the most handsome man in four counties, and he was cocky and full of life; swaggering from one weeping girl to the next without a care in the world. Which was of course how Connor himself had been only a few years ago – the swagger at least – back when the world had seemed fresh and new and full of endless possibility. Where had all that gone? He wondered, then pushed the thought away because the answer was all too obvious.

'You're looking tired, brother,' said Ryan, grabbing an

apple from a bowl of fruit and throwing it in the air like a hurling ball.

Connor gave a wry smile. 'Maybe you're right. It's been a big night so far.'

'I heard,' grinned Ryan, catching his apple and pulling a knife from the kitchen block. 'The Ross Oil woman. She's a looker, am I right?'

'That's as maybe,' said Connor, frowning. 'But what's important is what Ross Oil is going to do to the village.'

'Been playing the wet blanket again, have you?' Ryan expertly carved slices from the apple. Not only was Ryan part-time bar man and heartbreaker, he was also the pub's resident chef, something he had a genuine talent for, not that he had much interest in it. Ryan speared some apple on the end of the knife and offered it to his brother. Connor shook his head.

'Hey, I don't claim to know what's best for the Cove myself. I just think we need to think beyond the pot of gold. This is our home, Ryan. Yours too.'

There was a moment when the twinkle left his brother's eye, a frown creasing his brow.

'Is it, Con?' he said. 'Just because Clover Cove is your idea of paradise, don't assume it's the same for everyone else.'

'Paradise? Hardly.'

'Come on brother, you're practically the mayor of Clover Cove. You took over right where Dad left off.'

Connor turned on him, but Ryan just laughed that care-free laugh, dancing away his hands held up in surrender. 'Only joshing with you brother,' he chuckled, 'I just think it's a riot how you care so much about the Cove when only a few years ago, you couldn't stand the place. "First chance I get, Ryan," you said to me, "I'm getting the hell out of this hole."'

Connor glowered. 'People change,' he said.

'Oh, that they do,' said Ryan. 'But not all that much. The leopard can change his pyjamas, but never his spots, isn't that right?'

'So what would you have us do? Let the oil people come in with their bulldozers and push us into the sea?'

Ryan held up a hand and rubbed the tips of his fingers together. 'For the right price, you betcha. And don't tell me Dadda wouldn't have said the same thing. He'd have bitten their hands off.'

'Yeah, well Dad lived in different times. The fish had all gone, people were desperate for work. He would have been doing the best for the village as he saw it then.'

'So what's so different now? Mikey Carroll lives in the same tumbledown house he did then, Raff's old boat is the same one his father took to sea. They're still struggling.'

'But people don't need to go to Galway or Dublin to have a career anymore. They can work remotely or run an internet business.'

Ryan laughed.

'Not if you're a fisherman or a farmer.'

'Well diversify into tourism then.'

'Ah catch onto yersel, Con,' said Ryan. 'Who's booked your grand "spa suites" in the last four months? How many people are stopping at Molly's tea room by the harbor?'

He held up a curled finger and thumb to show 'zero'.

'At least people have a chance. If Mam was here...'

For the first time, Connor saw anger flare in his brother's eyes.

'But Mam isn't here, Con! They're gone and so is Ciara.'

Ciara. The name they dare not speak.

'What's she got to do with this?' said Connor quietly.

'*Everything*, you big fathead. You want everything to

stay the same so she'll come back. And if she doesn't, you want to keep hiding here.'

'I'm not hiding from anything. I just care about the Cove...'

Ryan's expression softened and he put one hand on Connor's shoulder.

'I know you do, brother. But you've got to let people make their own decisions. Make their own mistakes.'

'Like I did with Ciara, you mean?'

Ryan dropped his hand and let out an exasperated sigh.

'No, I'm saying Ciara made her choice and you have to live with that too, however much you might wish it was otherwise. And it, well, it doesn't look like she's going to change her mind now, does it? It's been two years, Con.'

Connor opened a cupboard and pulled out a pile of towels. He'd tired of the conversation.

'I've got work to do,' he said gruffly. 'Can you take on the bar for a while? You know we can't leave Raff in charge for too long.'

'Sure, no problem,' said Ryan, making an ironic salute. 'Just think about it, huh?'

'It's all I ever do,' he said, backing out the door. He slowly walked up the stairs towards the rooms. The pub had always been an inn since time immemorial. It was all part of the hospitality they offered. But Ryan was right: it was hardly used these days. Tourism wasn't exactly a boom industry; since the bypass had been built, people tended to head south to the ring of Kerry. And there was a good chance his little brother was right about the rest of it too. Maybe Connor's motivations weren't entirely altruistic. He *had* been hiding from the world, that was for sure. Ciara leaving and their father passing had come in quick succession, body blows that had left him doubled up. He had intended to stay to lick his wounds, but weeks had turned to months, months to years and here he still was. The boy who had wanted to conquer the world was now desperate to hold onto just one corner of it. But none of that meant he was wrong about the danger the Cove faced. He just had no idea how to fight the machine he feared was going to roll into the square.

He stopped outside the Ross girl's room, his knuckles raised to knock. He could hear a muffled voice. He frowned, listening: was she on the phone?

'Please hon...' he heard her say. 'I miss you...'

He froze as his foot found the one creaky board in the corridor. Leaving the towels outside the door, Connor quickly backed away, not entirely sure why he was feeling so disappointed.

Chapter 9

Kate frowned, throwing an arm over her face. It was so bright – how could it be so bright when it was still the middle of the night? Groaning, she turned over, trying to block the light with her pillow, but it was no use. She was awake now; wide awake in fact. Jetlag had always affected her horribly. Kate spent so many nights mornings sitting in hotel rooms, flicking through foreign TV channels or wandering through the deserted streets of unfamiliar towns and cities because her body clock kept waking her up at the wrong times.

The price you pay for a jet-setting lifestyle, she thought, rubbing her face with both hands sitting up on one elbow.

'Oh wow,' she said, squinting towards the window.

The light shining in her eyes was the rising sun, its deep orange rays glinting off the sea. The sash window, which had rattled and complained throughout the night, now framed a breathtaking vista of endless glass-flat ocean. Stretching, Kate padded to the window and looked out, her breath fogging the glass. *This* was why people came to Ireland. It was quite simply beautiful. Glancing at her watch she saw that was barely five. She would have the whole place to herself. With growing excitement, Kate pulled on her clothes and careful to make as little noise as possible, tiptoed down the stairs past the bar and out of a side door.

Wrapping her thin coat around her, Kate sucked in the cold air, a smile creeping onto her face. What a difference a few hours made. Where yesterday the village square had been grey and depressing, now it was magical. The road leading down towards the harbor was still wet from the night's rain but the sunlight slanting between the buildings made it sparkle. It was as if she was being led along a jeweled pathway in a children's fairy tale.

Beyond the square, a few terraced houses crowded into the steep single-track roadway, taking Kate down to the small harbor surrounded by a seawall, where a handful of rowboats and battered-looking launches were tied. Crumbling cliffs framed the cove on both sides and perched on the headland to her right was a tiny chapel, its grey stone and slate roof weathered by countless storms and yet still it stood, watching over the fishing boats as they came and went, generation after generation. Not that there was much fishing in Clover Cove anymore, Kate had done her research on that. The global economy and an over-fished sea had put paid to the viability of the industry. It was now far cheaper to catch cod, salmon and sea bass off Iceland, freeze it and ship it to China for processing, then ship it straight back to Molly's cafe for sale to fishermen like Raff. It was a prime reason Ross Oil was looking to Ireland as a base for its eco energy projects; the local economy needed them.

Of course, not everyone saw it that way. They never did.

The tide was out and Kate had to shield her eyes from the sun reflecting off the wet beach. Carefully walking down a seaweed-strewn slipway, Kate stepped onto the hard sand. Her first guess had been right: she was alone. Who else would be up at this hour? Besides a tangle of marks left by seagulls seeking the early worm, Kate's solitary footprints were the only sign that anything had passed this way. Just for a moment as she strode towards the sea, Kate allowed herself the fantasy of being the last woman on earth, sharing the planet only with the birds wheeling overhead and the fish in the sea. She shivered. It was meant to be liberating to feel one with nature, but she just felt cold and lonely.

Sure, if every other human suddenly blinked out of existence, it might well might solve her work problems – plus she could help herself to anything in the windows of Tiffany's or Prada, which would be nice. But who would you talk to? Who could you call when you were feeling down? Kate wasn't the kind of person who had hundreds of friends, and since her mom and sisters had moved to Florida to look after her grandfather, Kate had barely seen her family outside of Thanksgiving. But even so, she hated the idea of being alone. Kate supposed that was part of the reason she had come to Ireland, to find some of the roots her grandfather had always talked about. Kate had been brought up to see Ireland as the 'motherland', a dreamy faraway land of magic and legend. And now she was here? Standing at the edge of the water, the waves hissing up to her toes, Kate could certainly see the beauty; she loved this place, connected with its wildness. Everything was green and gold and rich and alive, the land seemed to somehow get inside you. It was exciting and vivid, but... she sighed, the cold breath puffing in front of her. Clove Cove wasn't hers, not yet anyway. She looked up, out to the horizon. Somewhere out there across the blue was New York, her real home. But how real was it? Standing here, Manhattan that seemed like the fantasy, made up of snapshots from a thousand movies and TV shows. Had any of it been real? And now David was a thing of the past, was there really anything for her there anymore?

A movement out at sea, a shadow moving from the right. Shielding her eyes, Kate saw it was a boat and standing at the rear was an unmistakable silhouette: Geoff Rafferty, the fisherman. Squinting, she could see he was waving at her. So there was some industry in fishing after all; as long as you were prepared to get up even earlier than jetlagged travelers.

'Hi!' she called, waving back, feeling slightly silly; Raff was obviously far too far away to hear her. But she liked the fact that someone was waving at her, that *someone* here was glad to see her. With a final wave, the boat turned and Raff disappeared into his little cabin. Still smiling, Kate turned and walked along the water's edge, taking in the beach and the shape of the land. She couldn't help seeing it with a professional eye, seeing the sweep of the sand, tracing the line of the headland, searching for a place to lay pipes or run cables. Which of course was why the villagers disliked her – they didn't want pipes or cables or ships docking in the harbor. They didn't want anything to change. And why would you want to change such a beautiful coastline? Why not leave it as it was? Did they really need this? Did anyone really need Ross Oil or any oil company to charge in and destroy everything they loved?

And this was why she was here and David was back in New York, thought Kate, stopping at the foot of the cliffs. David wouldn't be worrying his pretty little head about destroying the beauty of the headland, he would already have done a deal, bought up three miles of coastline and ordered bulldozers to flatten everything. Kate, meanwhile, thought about things too much, cared about people and places; not exactly the kind of attributes you looked for in an oil executive.

She looked up suddenly as she heard a sharp bark. A dog – some sort of terrier, she thought – was peering over the edge of the cliff.

'Hello down there!'

Kate was still wondering if Irish dogs had the power of speech when she saw another face peep over. 'Will you be the American girl?' said a man with red hair and matching cheeks.

'Yes, I suppose I must be,' said Kate, laughing nervously.

'That's grand. Stay there, we'll be down in a tick.'

Kate didn't have to wait long. There was a scrabbling and a shower of dirt as a little brown dog found its way down the cliff, then bounded up to Kate, barking happily.

'Oh, hey there little fella,' said Kate, reaching out hesitantly to pat the dog's head.

'That little fella's a girl,' said the man, jumping down beside the beast, 'But she won't hold that against you. Fiddle's the name – hers, not mine.'

He strode forward, his hand outstretched and Kate was shaking it before she noticed that the man was wearing black robes.

'You – you're the priest?' she stammered, immediately feeling foolish, but the cleric just laughed.

'What gave it away?' he grinned, fingering his black and white dog collar. 'Declan Kinnear, at your service. Call me Father Dec, everyone does – not that I'm technically a father.'

'I'm sorry?' said Kate, confused. 'But you *are* a priest?'

'Oh yes, but a reverend, not a father.'

Clearly seeing Kate's confusion, the man smiled.

'Church of Ireland,' he said. 'I have a church, services on Sundays, carols at Christmas, all that. And I have the dog-collar too – both kinds. But our church is Church of Ireland, not Roman Catholic, so I'm a vicar – a reverend. The Catholics call their priests 'father' and it's gotten so ingrained in Ireland that any priest gets called 'father'. At least in Clover Cove they do.'

'I see,' said Kate, utterly confused.

He shrugged and laughed a jolly laugh.

'Don't worry, all my friends call me Dec. And you are Miss O'Riordan I take it? From the oil company?'

'I am, for my sins.'

'Well I hope there will be plenty of those,' smiled Father Dec, 'Between you and I, the gossip in the Cove has gotten a little stale of late. Nothing more racy than a few Euros in the swear box for ages.'

Kate had to do a double take of the man's face before she saw the twinkle in his eye.

'You're joking,' she said with relief.

'Just a little, Miss O'Riordan.'

'Kate, please,' she said. 'Seeing as we're on first name terms and all, Father Dec.'

'Kate then,' he smiled. He had an open, happy face, surprisingly good-looking and young for a priest; but then Kate reminded herself that was more of her Hollywood thinking. According to the movies, Irish priests were always white haired and craggy, weren't they? But there was no reason a young man couldn't take the vows, even a handsome one.

She felt herself blushing, but Father Dec was looking the other way, flinging a piece of driftwood for Fiddle the dog, who set off after it with a delighted yelp.

'Shall we walk?' he said, setting off back towards the headland. 'I love this time of day, don't you? So pretty with sun just rising.' He glanced across at her. 'But then you'll be planning on wrecking all this won't you Kate?'

Her heart sank. Kate had been counting on getting support from at least some of the local leaders. There was no logical reason that the priest should support the coming of a large-scale building project in the area – possibly quite the opposite – but it was still a blow.

'We have no plans to wreck anything, Father,' she said, her anger and frustration rising. 'Actually, we have no plans at all so far. I am simply here to look at the possibilities and talk to the local people about whether they would be open to us building something here.'

The priest simply looked at her, his eyebrows raised. Kate knew there was no point in alienating the man further, but her frustration had been building since the moment she had arrived in the Cove and she couldn't hold it back any longer.

'I'm sorry Father, but Ross Oil isn't some terrible ogre,' she said. 'If we did come to Clover Cove, we'd do so sympathetically and in full consultation with the local community. In fact, the project we've been looking at is in the generation of eco energy. No oil, no pipelines, and crucially, plenty of work for the people of the area.'

'Tidal stream generators, is it?' said the priest casually and Kate stopped dead in her tracks.

'Yes... how, how did you know?'

'I wasn't always a priest, Kate,' he smiled, tapping his chest with a cocked thumb. 'I was in the Royal Engineers for many years, but before that I scratched a degree in engineering from Trinity College, Dublin.'

'You're an engineer?'

'You'd be surprised how well theology and science mixes. My professor taught me that engineers have to respect the land, the sea and the almighty – if they don't, the Lord will laugh at them and everything will be washed away by the morning. It's fine advice in building and life both.'

Kate was still gaping at him, but Father Dec was gazing out to sea.

'I take it you're not considering a barrage array? More like a tidal fence?'

'Yes,' said Kate. 'Individual turbines like you have with wind farms, but under the water, anchored to the seabed, moving with the rise and fall of the tides.'

'So minimum impact on the environment?'

'Well, there's plenty of variables to look at first, but that's the idea. You'd only see the tops of the turbine poles peeping above the sea.'

Father Dec nodded.

'Well then, you don't have any problems,' he said.

Kate let out a laugh. 'Sorry Father, I wish that were true. No one wants me here and I can't really go back to New York unless I can convince them.'

The priest turned to look at her.

'Then convince them,' he said.

Kate raised a skeptical eyebrow.

'That easy?'

He gave her a thin smile.

'The decisions when there's no alternative are always the easy ones. War taught me that much.' And before Kate could say anything else, Father Dec turned away, whistling for Fiddle, who turned from where she had been playing at the water's edge and sprinted back towards her master.

'Oh and Kate?' he called, swivelling on his heel. 'If you get stuck, go and visit the chapel.'

She looked towards the headland, the tiny stone building perched above the waves.

'I think you'll find it helps,' he called.

'Yeah,' Kate whispered to herself. 'I could do with it.'

Chapter 10

The village was still quiet. Out in the fields, Farmer Garvey would be walking his cows out to pasture or feeding his ducks, but here in the square it was silent except for the squawk of the gulls out towards the water. Connor sat on the step of the pub and sipped his tea. It was one of his secret pleasures, getting up before the village stirred, the sun just peeking over the chapel but still a chill in the air. At this time, he felt as if the village was his alone, a secret jewel he could hold in his hand and savor its beauty. He'd learnt this from his father. Da always said early morning was the only time of day when no one wanted anything from you but the Almighty.

The thought made him turn to look up at the church tower. But wasn't it grand, pointing up to the heavens? Or was it the other way around: a ray of divine light falling from the sky? Years ago, Connor's father had fallen out with the parish priest and for a while things had soured between pub and church; always an awkward thing in Ireland where bar and altar were the two pillars of the community. But while another great Irish tradition was the ability to hold a grudge for centuries, Connor had never ceased to think of the church as anything other than good: a place of song and light and Christmas and weddings and yes, even funerals. He didn't often go to church himself, but Connor loved how there was a continuity and a solidity to it. Plus, that was where his Da was; his headstone at least.

He was just thinking about strolling over to visit the graveyard when there was a rumble as a truck rolled into the square.

'There's the man of the hour!' called the driver, leaning out the window.

'And it's yourself, Bryan', said Connor, reaching up to shake the man's hand. 'Bright and early I see.'

The driver killed the engine and jumped down from the cab. 'Other way round, Con, this is the end of my shift. Been working through the night, all up the coast from Cork. Four kids under six, y'see,' he shrugged. 'I need that double time.'

Bryan White had been driving 'the wagons' up and down the west coast since he was old enough to hold a heavy goods licence; it was in the blood; his father had delivered to the pub back when it was known as 'Cormac's'.

'And how are the little scamps?'

The true answer to that was 'unfortunate-looking' and 'a pain in the behind'; Connor often saw their tired mother Lara dragging them across the square on their noisy way to the little nursery school, but Bryan's eyes lit up at their mention.

'Ah, they're angels, Con. Pure angels. You know Liam, my eldest, he's playing the piano already. Proper little genius I've got there.'

'Of course, look at the raw DNA he's working with.'

Smiling, Bryan rolled up the back of the van. 'Here you are: fish, eggs, bread, all the usual. Plus,' he added, slapping a pile of shrink-wrapped pallets. 'Two dozen of those fancy lagers you asked for.'

'Ach, that's grand Bryan,' said Connor, clapping the man on the shoulder. 'Even out here they're asking for those craft beers, IPA and whatnot. You're a life saver, sure and you are.'

He reached for the first case, but Bryan blocked him by raising a clipboard.

'Small matter of the bill first,' he said, regret in his voice. 'Not for me, you understand, but Mr. McCann gets jumpy if the "i"s aren't dotted and the "t"s crossed.'

'Sure, no problem,' said Connor, patting his pockets. 'D'ya have a pen? I'll sign it off.'

Bryan shook his head.

'Nothing on the slate anymore, Con. The boss was very clear on that. Cash or check only.'

'Ah, that's no problem at all,' said Connor, slipping his arm around Bryan's shoulders. 'You come on inside while I find my check book, hmm?'

He felt the delivery man resist. 'I'd love to, Con, but Lara's expecting me back.'

'Sure and I'm not stopping you,' said Connor, gently steering Bryan through into the bar. 'But a man needs an eye-opener when he's been out with the owls, isn't that so?'

'You know I'd like nothing more, but...'

'Well you can't stand about while I write this check, can you? Have a seat at least.'

But Connor was already pouring a brandy, the good stuff he kept under the counter for emergencies just like this. He watched the driver's eyes, following the amber liquid gurgling into the glass, watched the man licking his lips.

'One won't hurt now, will it?' smiled Connor. 'End of your shift. You've earned it.'

'Now Con, Lara won't see it that way.'

Connor shrugged and slid the glass across and held his hands open, a gesture that said, 'up to you.'

Con wouldn't usually have played on Bryan's well-known love of a brandy, but he happened to know that Bryan's wife Lara would prefer Bryan kept out of the house. Having spent the night separated from his little ones, Bryan would bash through the door, handing out sweets and giving piggy-back rides, whipping the kids into a frenzy. Then he'd crash out, worn out from work and play, leaving Lara to pick up the pieces. At least this way Bryan would zonk out in his armchair and Lara would get the kids to nursery without any meltdowns.

Bryan hissed with pleasure as the first drink went down and Connor refilled the glass. Now had to do was figure how to get the van unloaded without Bryan drinking the whole bottle.

As if on cue, Grace walked through the door. Pretty, red-haired and feisty, Grace was Connor's secret weapon. Just the right combination of friendly and no-nonsense, Grace was the perfect barmaid, aside from the fact she was too bright to stay very long.

'Ah, my favorite girl,' cooed Bryan, waving his already empty glass in greeting. 'Will you join me in a drink, Gracie?'

Grace glanced at Connor and instantly understood his raised eyebrows.

'Isn't the lovely Mrs. White your favorite girl?' she smiled at Bryan.

'Ah, and so she is,' said Bryan, his eyes sparkling. 'She's an angel too.'

'Bryan's been working through the night,' said Connor nodding towards the brandy meaningfully. 'He's just unwinding.'

‘Ah so,’ nodded Grace, refilling his glass. ‘Then we’d bet get you unwound, hadn’t we?’

‘I’ll just get that stuff from the van, Bryan,’ said Connor and smiled as the driver waved a hand, all thoughts of a check forgotten. It wouldn’t take long to take the boxes through into the kitchen; the Suites and Spa wasn’t exactly overflowing with guests so their catering needs were light. Even so, Connor was three months behind on the bills and his cashflow wasn’t likely to take a sharp upswing, unless someone saw fit to shift Christmas a few months early. The truth was he was getting worried. Connor’s was a Clover Cove institution, sure, but it was still a business. And as a business, it was in danger of failing.

He heard the door open and turned. The Ross woman, her cheeks pink.

‘Good morning,’ she said, primly.

‘An early walk around the village, is it?’

‘Jetlag,’ said Kate O’Riordan. ‘My body doesn’t know if it’s day or night.’

The mention of Kate O’Riordan’s body made Connor look away, awkwardly shifting the sack in his arms.

‘Say, I just met your priest,’ said Kate, filling the silence. ‘Father Dec, was it?’

‘Indeed it is.’ A smile crept onto Connor’s face. ‘And how was Fiddle?’

‘The dog? She was cute.’ The woman frowned. ‘Why do you ask?’

‘Ah, then you passed the test.’

‘Test?’

‘Well now, Fiddle’s like the village guard dog. If she doesn’t like the smell of you, she’s liable to go for your ankles.’

The American looked shocked. ‘Not very holy.’

‘God moves in mysterious ways, doesn’t he now?’

'Let's hope so, Mr. James,' said Kate and walked up the stairs. He watched, enjoying the sway of her. Then sighing, Connor returned to the van to pick up the beer.

'Need a hand?'

Con turned to see Mikey Carroll standing awkwardly at the kerb.

'Sure Mikey,' smiled Connor. 'Always glad to swear in a deputy.'

Mikey had been the village blacksmith – or rather, he still was, having inherited the forge and the business from his father – but people didn't need horseshoes and plowshares and wagon axles anymore and they could get gates and garden furniture from the Swedish warehouse place out towards Kilmara. Mikey wasn't the brightest bauble in the box, but he had a big heart and arms like knotted rope, and like many people in Clover Cove, was struggling to make ends meet.

'Just put the beer in the back room, you know where they go.'

As he passed, Connor slipped a note into Mikey's shirt pocket. *Easy come, easy go,* he thought.

'And when you've finished,' he called, 'go see Grace in the bar, I'll get her to make you a sandwich.'

'Connor James.'

A greeting and a statement. He turned to see Mrs. Brennan, the florist. Or rather the village's unofficial florist, given she didn't have a shop any more.

'Good to see you well, Mrs. Brennan,' said Connor, tipping an imaginary hat. 'And how's your Karen? I hear she's head of the company now.'

The old lady gave a small smile. 'Not quite, but she's doing very well. Her boss just gave her a raise, said she was invaluable.'

Connor watched Diana Brennan's chest swell. Part of a

landlord's job was to know his clientele, even if they didn't drink at the bar. Mrs. Brennan disapproved of alcohol, but pride was her poison, particularly in her daughter who had some sort of high-flying job out in Dublin. Danny, her son, was the local news hound, but Karen was the apple of her eye.

'And how's the flower business?'

The woman's mouth turned downwards.

'No good?' asked Connor, 'I thought you'd had a good month. Wasn't there that big wedding and poor Mr. Haye's funeral?'

The woman pursed wrinkled lips.

'Taxes, Connor. It's my end of year.'

'Ah, I see. Annoying.'

'More than annoying,' she said, a hitch in her voice. 'I really don't see how I'm going to pay.'

Connor briefly entertained the idea of suggesting the woman ask her successful daughter to help, but he knew a woman of Mrs. Brennan's generation would rather starve than ask for a handout.

'Well it's fortunate I've caught you,' said Connor, 'I've been meaning to talk to you about the pub.'

'The pub?'

'Well, as you know, my folks ran it in the traditional way, which was fine, but lately I've been trying to modernize the old place. We've revamped the hotel upstairs, for example.'

'You have a spa, I hear?'

A spa that consisted of two badly plumbed whirlpool baths and some fancy-smelling bodywash on the sink.

'Exactly, so I was wondering if you would be willing to help with the decor?'

She eyed the pub's door as if he were asking her to jump into bed with the devil himself.

'Help how?' she said suspiciously.

'Well, in those fancy hotels in Dublin and Paris, they have big flower displays in the lobby, don't they? I was thinking maybe we could do something similar, maybe on the bar and on the tables?'

He pulled out his check book. 'And given it's to be a regular thing, I'd be prepared to pay in advance.'

Her chin lifted.

'That's not necessary, Connor.'

He smiled and waggled the pages of the book. 'I'm assuming I'll be getting a discount.'

They thrashed out the details: petunias and roses and nasturtiums, foliage depending on availability. Mrs. Brennan insisted on weekly changes and Connor held out until she agreed to provide the vases. They both parted smiling, but Connor's grin faded as soon as Diana Brennan left the square. He'd made her happy and kept a local service in business, but he could ill afford philanthropy. He might be able to head off Bryan the driver with a few drinks, but Bryan's boss wouldn't be so easily deflected. And then there was the electric, the water, the backed up credit for the mixers and the wiring that was threatening to fry anyone who dared brave the cellar. A movement caught his eye and he turned to see the American woman standing at her bedroom window. Raising her eyebrows, she pulled the window shut with a thud.

Connor sighed. Maybe Ryan was right. Maybe selling out to the oil company was the smart move. Connor wasn't even all that sure why he was so resistant to the proposal beyond some vague feeling that Clover Cove might lose something important.

He turned to look back at the church.

'If you were thinking of sending me a sign, boss,' he said. 'Now might be a good time.'

Chapter 11

Kate lay back in the bath, wriggling her toes. The pipes in the wall had complained, but at least the water was good and hot, which meant the feeling had come back into her extremities. The beach had been beautiful, but it had been cold. Manhattan in winter could be bitter, with the wind funneling down the concrete canyons, but at least in New York there was always a coffee shop or a subway to duck into. Plus she had packed in a hurry, bringing clothes appropriate for business meetings, not icy beach walks. She lifted a wrinkled finger and blew a cloud of bubbles in the air. She hadn't packed a warm coat, but she had remembered to bring a bottle of her favorite bath oil; the luxurious mound of foam covering her body reminded her of civilization and was always a guaranteed mood-lifter. Her conversation with Father Dec had also helped. He hadn't been welcoming exactly, but he'd taken her seriously. And he had been right: if you had no choice, it actually put you in a position of strength. Kate might be facing a hostile crowd, but at least her back was against the wall – and when your back was against the wall, you could only go forward. There was no way she would go crawling back to New York, not when she could imagine the look of triumph on David's face, and anyway, she had hardly even started in Clover Cove yet. Just because the pub's landlord had taken a dislike to her, it didn't mean the whole village was against her. Once she explained the company's plans and benefits to the local area, she was confident that they would...

'Knock knock.'

Kate froze, her eyes wide. The voice had come from just outside the bathroom door. *Inside* her bedroom.

'Who is it?' she called, 'I'm in the bath.'

'It's Connor,' came the reply, then a pause. 'The landlord.'

'I know who you *are*,' snapped Kate, 'What I want to know is what you're doing in my room!'

She had tried for outrage, but her voice had come out as a thin wail, like a lady in those regency romances she'd read as a child. Then Kate followed the wail with a gasp as Connor's head appeared around the door.

'HEY!' Kate cried, lunging for a towel and just managing to cover herself. 'What on earth are you doing?'

Connor was holding up one hand and in the other was what looked like a spanner. Both eyes were screwed shut. 'Don't fret yerself,' she said, 'I'm not looking or anything. I just need to get to the water tank.'

'What? What water tank?'

Eyes still closed, he fumbled along the bathroom wall until his hands found a cupboard next to the sink. 'This happens when someone has a bath,' he said, 'Airlock in the pipes, stops the rest of us getting any hot water and I need to get on with the breakfast.'

'I'm sorry, but this is just unacceptable!' said Kate.

'Oh, I know,' said Connor, grunting as he clanked his spanner against the pipes, 'It's your man Raff again. Never should have trusted him to fix the plumbing. But he's cheap.'

'CONNOR!' she shouted.

'What?' Evidently engrossed in his task, he turned towards her, eyes open. Letting out a sharp shriek, Kate slipped down under the bubbles, sending a wave of hot water slopping onto the floor. Connor, remembering he wasn't supposed to look, quickly turned away and, his feet slipping on the suds, fell forward, banging his head on the open cupboard door.

'OWW!' he cried, dropping the spanner to clutch his forehead, his hand coming away covered in blood. Groaning, he slipped face-down onto the floor.

'Connor? Are you okay?'

He didn't move.

'Oh my...' Keeping the wet towel firmly in position, Kate scrabbled awkwardly to her feet and grabbed her robe, quickly belting it around her. Splashing more water onto the floor as she jumped out of the bath, she knelt by the prone man, her heart in her mouth. What if he was badly injured? What if he was *dead*?

'Connor? Oh Connor, I'm so sorry!'

'I should bloody hope so too,' he said, immediately sitting up.

'You're... you're okay?'

He touched the cut on his brow gingerly. 'No, I'm not *okay*,' he said, glaring at her. 'Look at my head! What did you do that for?'

'What did *I* do...?' snapped Kate, '*You* were the one who came sneaking into my bathroom when I was completely naked!'

Connor's eyes shifted to her bare knees.

'You're naked?'

'Not now, but I WAS!' She said, quickly stepping back

and pulling another towel in front of her. 'How do *you* bathe?'

'With the door locked,' said Connor, clambering to his feet.

'I didn't think I needed to lock it,' said Kate, crossing her arms defiantly. 'I assumed I'd have privacy, this being my private spa and all.'

Connor gave a cynical smile.

'This is Clover Cove, Miss. The local dialect has no word for "privacy."'

'I'm not from Clover Cove,' she said, raising her chin.

Connor's dark, mischievous eyes took her in, her silk robe clinging to her wet body and a smirk slid onto his mouth.

'Aye, I can see that.' He held her gaze for a fraction of a second, then added. 'Breakfast, ten minutes.'

Before she could respond, he turned and walked out.

Kate stood there, watching the space he had vacated, her mouth wide open.

Chapter 12

The girl had quite the appetite, thought Connor approvingly, peeking through the serving hatch as Kate sat back in her chair and sipped her post-breakfast tea. Any girl who could cope with the notorious 'Full English' breakfast was to be admired, but the Irish Breakfast – *whoo boy* – that took it one stage further. Add Ryan's skill in the kitchen and the whole thing became almost an art form. He had plied Kate with poached eggs, sausages, crispy bacon, grilled tomatoes, mushrooms and beans, all laid on top of a slab of fried bread. He thought they might have her with the white pudding, a sliced sausage made mostly of pig's blood, but from what he could see, she had polished that off too.

'She's asking if we have any jelly for the toast,' said Grace, dropping Kate's empty plate in the kitchen sink, 'I think she means marmalade.'

She turned to Ryan, who was cleaning his hard-worked frying pan, 'She also said she thought the fried bread would probably be illegal in California. I think it was meant as a compliment. Oh, and she said your eggs were perfect.'

Connor and Ryan exchanged raised eyebrows,

Connor's appreciation of the girl growing. Ryan had learnt to cook from their mother who had been very clear about how a fried breakfast should be cooked. Eggs should be firm to the touch, but with a runny centre, the bacon crisp, tomato grilled, never fried. And the tea, of course, had to be so strong it could melt the spoon.

'She asked to see you,' said Grace, giving Connor a knowing smile.

'I think someone's sweet on you, Con,' said Ryan with a wink.

Connor shook his head, wiping his hands on his apron. 'More like she wants to complain about me peeking at her in the bath.'

'You were... *what*?' gasped Grace, but Connor was already half through the door.

'Enjoyed your food, I see,' said Connor as he approached the table. Kate, as the sole resident of the Spa and Suites, was the only customer in the bar before opening.

'It's the sea air, I think,' said Kate. 'Plus I haven't eaten since the plane. And you know how appetizing airline food is.'

'No, actually,' said Connor. 'How is it?'

Kate frowned. 'You've never eaten on an airplane?'

'Never been on an aeroplane,' said Connor, leaning on the back of a chair.

She blinked.

'Never?'

'Never. It's funny, when I was younger, I always thought I'd travel all over the world, but somehow I never got there. Imagine all that jet-setting's pretty glamorous though, eh?'

Kate snorted. 'Not really, it wears you out. In my industry, you have to travel a lot – places like Norway or the Middle East. I was in Alaska in June.'

Connor whistled. 'That does sound glamorous. I read a lot of Jack London when I was a boy. All those Huskies and gold mines. Aye, that sounded grand.'

Kate smiled to herself. 'Yes, I guess it might sound fun, but the reality is a lot of airports and waiting in line, a heap of sticky taxi cabs, staying for a meeting then flying straight back, writing some report on the tray table, trying not to jab someone with my elbows.'

Connor laughed and wagged a finger at her. 'Ah, you almost had me for a moment there.'

'Well, I guess there's an upside,' said Kate. 'I'm something of an expert on Matt Damon movies – there's always one showing on the in-flight entertainment system, wherever in the world you are.'

The girl liked action flicks too, she was getting better and better. He had to remind himself she wasn't here as a tourist.

'Haven't you ever been abroad?' she asked.

Connor pouted, thinking.

'Does Galway count? Oh, and I went to Dublin once. Noisy it was.'

'Why not? I mean, you said you wanted to see the world.'

He gave a smile, raising one eyebrow.

'What are you doing this morning?' he asked.

Kate glanced at her watch.

'Well, I have an appointment at ten.'

Connor nodded.

'With Sir Charles Balcon, at Sleagh Castle.'

Kate started. 'Do people in this village really know everything about everyone else?'

Connor laughed. 'I'm not a magician,' he said. 'His

Lordship's land touches the coast to the south, so I reckoned he'd be one of the first people you'd want to speak to.'

Kate tilted her head, as if she was reassessing him. Her gaze made him feel uncomfortable.

'Listen, how about I walk you up there?' he asked quickly. 'It's not far to the castle along the cliffs and there's something I want to show you on the way.'

'I... ah...'

Connor almost laughed at the woman's reaction. She'd make a terrible card player. She was clearly thinking, 'What is he up to?' Then again, he could hardly blame the girl when he'd been so hostile the night before.

He held up his hands in surrender. 'No agenda here, I promise. Well, not much. Just helping you out is all.'

There was a moment's pause, then she smiled. She was cute when she wasn't frowning all the time, thought Connor, then squashed the thought.

'Sure, why not?' said Kate. 'When do you want to leave?'

He pulled at the bow of his apron and tossed it onto the bar. 'I'm suddenly free now.'

'Why? What's happened?'

'I should be washing the dishes, but there's no hot water.'

Chapter 13

Kate had to trot to keep up. Connor set quite a pace, striding ahead in his green waxed jacket and Wellingtons. *Where's the fire?* She thought as she did her best to follow. At least Connor had thought to lend her a puffer jacket and a pair of gumboots apparently left by a barmaid last winter. The boots were still at least two sizes too large, flopping against her shins, but it was a marked improvement on the two choices in her suitcase: four-inch heels or fashion house sneakers, neither of which would have got her much beyond the village square. A path led from the side of the pub, winding past the backs of buildings and out into a quiet lane with high hedges on both sides. 'Over the stile here,' said Connor, vaulting up onto a little wooden staircase next to a gate.

'A stile?'

'It's a little ladder we build for the leprechauns,' said Connor, face deadpan. He held out a hand to help Kate, but she grasped the fence instead and stepped over.

'Suit yerself,' he said as he led her diagonally across a field. At the last moment, the field dipped and there was the sea, bruise-blue and moody as Connor's eyes. *I'm making comparisons with his eyes now?* Thought Kate, annoyed with herself.

Connor stopped, hand shading his brow as he gazed out over the water.

'Now wouldja look at that?' he sighed. 'Why would a person need to leave this place when God's own country is just outside his door?'

'It is lovely, I can't deny that,' said Kate. 'But there are other beautiful places too.'

'Oh yeah?' said Connor sceptically. 'Where?'

Kate laughed, but she could see he wasn't joking.

'The world's a big place, Connor. Okay, how about the pyramids in Egypt? Wouldn't you like to see one of the wonders of the world?'

'Too hot. Dusty too, I'm guessing.'

'Well how about Mount Everest? Nepal or Tibet; they're cool enough. I went trekking in Nepal a few years ago, it was stunning.'

He shrugged.

'Don't like heights much.'

'The fjords of Norway then. You could stay in the boat.'

'I'm sure it's nice, but have you seen the sun set over Loch Corrib?'

Kate looked at him skeptically.

'Have you?'

'No, but there's nothing like a sunset over the chapel,' he said, turning back towards the harbor. 'Ah, when the light slants across the rock, I swear it's like the good lord's smiling down at us.'

She looked at him, wondering if he was serious or teasing her for fun. She certainly wasn't sure she had ever met someone with no desire to see the world before. How could you make such a statement about the beauty of a sunset – however stunning – if you had never seen another?

She watched him head off along the cliffs, his broad back almost part of the landscape. And perhaps that was it: people like Connor connected with the place they lived in, became as much a part of it as the rocks and the heather and the sand. And why? For no other reason than it was their home, the place they belonged. She thought of her grandfather and instantly felt lonely again.

Connor had stopped at the edge of a steep drop and Kate followed him carefully, peering over the edge. Stark granite plunged downwards, dragon's teeth of volcanic rock jutting in and out of the boiling sea below.

'Ironship bay,' said Connor.

'Strange name.'

He nodded.

'Well it was called something else – Sea Cave Cove, something like that – until the Germans started wrecking their ships on the rocks in the Great War. The story is a whole fleet of the Kaiser's Dreadnoughts went down one night, every hand lost.'

'Is it deep?' asked Kate warily, resisting the urge to clutch Connor's arm.

'No one knows,' said Connor, 'There's a local story that some old ship's captain was in the pub and he made a bet he could measure the depth here in fathoms, so got his crew to throw an anchor off the cliff and see how much of the chain played out.'

'What happened?'

'Apparently the long end got caught around his ankle and he was pulled in. No one ever saw the anchor or the captain again.'

Kate glanced at him, once again not sure if she were

being gently mocked or whether this was standard Irish blarney, their penchant for telling tall tales.

'Is this what you wanted to show me?'

'No, it's down here.' He jumped over a hummock of grass and Kate gasped as he landed on a narrow shelf below. He turned and held up both hands towards her. 'Now this time you'll have to let me ease you down,' he said firmly. 'Assuming your modern prinicples will allow it.'

'My modern...?' she gasped. What year was this? Bristling, Kate stepped to the side and, avoiding Connor's outstretched arms, clambered awkwardly down on her own. She wasn't going to let some male chauvinist baby her.

Shrugging, Connor turned and disappeared around the outcrop. Gritting her teeth, Kate followed, trying not to look down at the crashing waves too much, but it was hard not to have a glance every now and then. She found that she was holding her breath without realising. Finally, she limped around to where Connor was waiting by a deep crack in the rock.

'Here we are now,' said Connor in a low voice. 'Try not to move sudden-like.'

He gestured towards a flat boulder below an overhang, indicating that she should sit next to him. Reluctantly, Kate shuffled over until their hips were touching. Looking out, it felt like they were inside the cliffs, with a sea cave right below them where the waves would rush inside, then explode against the rock and pound out again. Kate could feel the spray settling on her skin.

'Now then, you see the big shadow to the left of the cave?' said Connor, leaning so close to Kate she could feel his heat. She swallowed and nodded.

'Okay, so look just below where the tufts of sea grass are growing, there's a little hole in the ledge. See?'

'Oh my heavens!' gasped Kate as she saw movement on

the ledge and a small black bird emerged. It had a white chest and big slanted eyes, which were looking curiously at them both. It looked like an angry penguin. But that wasn't the most striking thing about it. That honor belonged to the bird's beak, squat and curved like a parakeet, mostly orange but with vivid stripes of red, black and yellow.

'What is it?' whispered Kate.

'That's a puffin,' grinned Connor. 'Strangest and prettiest bird on the west coast.'

As they watched, more puffins appeared, a whole family it seemed, each of them with this strange, odd, beautiful bill and almost comical bright orange feet.

'Now aren't they wonderful?'

'Oh yes. Yes they are.'

Connor pointed out other birds huddled on the cliffs or wheeling overhead. Kittiwakes, guillemots, razorbills and fulmars. There was even a sinister-looking black thing improbably called a 'shag', bobbing on the surface, preening its oily feathers with a long beak and studiously ignoring a family of otters floating barely feet away. Kate was mesmerized. It was as if a soothing landscape painting had been brought to life by the hustle and bustle of nature, the peace of where the stone met the water only broken by the hollow boom of waves in the cave and the cry and conversation of the birds over the low whisper of the wind.

She glanced over at Connor and it was the first time Kate had seen his face really soften. It was like clouds parting to let the sunlight through. She could tell he loved this wild place, was proud of it – and she understood why he had brought her here. Not to impress her with its beauty, but to show her what might be lost.

'Thank you,' she said quietly.

He looked at her, his brow instantly furrowed, his eyes guarded again.

'What for?'

Suddenly Kate felt awkward, wrong-footed, as if she had said too much or broken some spell. She gestured at the sea and the cliffs.

'For showing me this.'

Connor's lips parted and he looked like he was about to respond, but simply nodded and rose, patting the dust from his hands.

'You'll be late for his Lordship,' he said.

He led her back along the cliff and up onto the main path in silence, his back to Kate, striding on ahead, compounding her feeling that she had done or said the wrong thing. Step by step, her irritation grew. Connor James was maddening; all she had wanted to do was thank him for the gesture, but he had just made her feel stupid and rude. God, she hated men – people – like that.

By the time she had caught up with him at the top of the hill, irritation had turned to anger. Kate knew her face was burning; it had always done that, ever since she was a girl when she was embarrassed or furious, but Connor James seemed oblivious.

'There you go,' he said, nodding towards the big house. 'Sleagh Castle. Word of advice, best not tell Sir Charles that you're single.'

Her eyes grew wide. The arrogance of the man!

'How do you know I'm single?' she snapped.

He looked down at her hands, ringless.

'Unwed, then.'

She put her hands on her hips and glared at him. Did he really think an unmarried woman couldn't look after herself? Did he think she shouldn't have a job? He was unbearable!

'I think I'll be fine, thank you,' she said through tight lips.

He raised a skeptical eyebrow. 'Fair enough. Just follow the path back the same way, it's hard to get lost.'

'Aren't you coming to the house?'

He smiled. 'I don't think it'd help your cause,' he said. 'Sir Charles and I... we have history. Wouldn't want him thinking we were pals.'

Are we pals? thought Kate immediately, feeling oddly both elated and let down. Pals was good, it meant he hadn't been offended by her earlier faux pas. But it also meant, well, that they were *just* pals. *Not that it's a bad thing*, she thought, reminding herself that Connor was sexist and rude and insufferable.

'But where...' she began, turning to see that Connor was already walking down the path and her words had been snatched away by the wind.

'Fine,' she muttered to herself and turned towards the house. She didn't need Connor James. Ginny had been right: she didn't need a man. And she certainly didn't need Connor James.

Chapter 14

Connor strode down the field, his jaw tight. *Oh, well handled,* he thought angrily. *First you terrify the poor girl, then you insult her, make her think you're some sort of neanderthal.*

He stopped and turned, looking back towards the big house, but Kate O'Riordan had gone. He let out a long breath and rubbed a hand over his mouth.

What was that crack about her 'modern principles'? He'd meant to make the point that in Clover Cove, equality was a given because everyone had to help one another, but instead he'd obviously come across as a sexist throwback.

'Well played, Connor,' he whispered. Great first impression he was making.

Not that it was his job to look after the Ross Oil woman; he was the landlord of the pub, not the head of the local tourist board. But after his spiky welcome last night, Connor had decided that hostility wasn't the answer, not towards Kate O'Riordan anyway. Softly, softly, catchy monkey and all that. Ross Oil was big, powerful and rich and if they tried to fight toe-to-toe, little Clover Cove would just get crushed under the treads of the Ross Oil bulldozers – or their legal team. No, the village needed to box clever and wait for the right moment to come off the ropes, and until then he knew it was smart to stop antagonising Miss O'Riordan.

Which was why he had suggested the excursion to Ironship Bay. Connor knew his limits: he didn't have Ryan's smooth charm or Raff's disarming way with people. But he knew that if Kate O'Riordan saw the puffins in their nests and watched the cormorants diving for fish, if she could sit on the cliffs and see this land the way he did, then she might think twice about changing anything.

That had been the theory. In reality, she probably thought his plan was to take her up to the cliffs to push her over. He had seen the way she had clung to the rocks like a woman about to do her first bungee jump.

He gave a gentle snort. *Ah, but she was game, wasn't she?* he thought admiringly. Terrified though she was, she'd still edged her way along that path, refusing to take his hand. She had a fire, that one.

And she *had* seen the beauty, Connor was sure of it. So why had he made that dumb comment about how she wasn't married? Like that was any of his business!

He shook his head and looked out to sea.

'Messed it up again, Da,' he whispered.

He walked down to the edge of the field and found the little path down to the beach and strode across the sand, enjoying the breeze ruffling his hair. He stopped at the water's edge and waited for the foam-topped waves to lap up to his toes, skipping back just out of reach like a child at the seaside. Connor bent to pick up a pretty mussel shell, turning it so it caught the light, the blues and purples flashing. He didn't get down here nearly enough, where you could smell the sea and feel the sand under your fingertips; too much time in the bar, listening to tall tales.

He heard a shout and turned to see a small figure on the harbor wall, waving. Even from this distance he could recognize the silhouette of his brother.

'Hey Ryan!'

Ryan beckoned and Connor jogged over, meeting him at the foot of the lane.

'Came looking for you,' said Ryan. 'You're needed up at the bar. Grace said you'd gone off with the Ross woman.'

Connor nodded non-committally.

'What's the craic?'

'Trouble, looks like. We had Shaun O'Neal, the guy from the dairy banging on the door.'

Connor's heart sank. He'd been expecting something like this.

'Shaun was all worked up and red in the face, saying we're way behind on some invoice he sent three weeks ago. I smoothed things over a little, but he still said he won't deliver our milk until it's paid.'

Connor blew his cheeks out.

'Better get used to having our coffee black then.'

Ryan gave him a sideways look.

'Why dontcha just pay?'

'It's complicated. Cashflow problems.'

They had reached the square and he walked back through the pub's kitchen door, Ryan following. There was an invoice sitting on the counter, emblazoned with a blood red 'OVERDUE' stamp. Connor snatched it up and stuffed it into a drawer along with all the other angry bills.

'So was that what your walk with pretty Kate was about? Money? Have you decided to give the people their way?'

Connor thumped the drawer shut.

'The people? What are you, Trotsky all of a sudden?'

Ryan held up both hands, a sly grin on his face. 'Not me, Comrade: Trotsky ended up getting assassinated. Besides, I'm the one man in the village who this doesn't affect, so I'm Switzerland in this war.'

Connor frowned. 'Why doesn't it affect you? Ross Oil's plans effect everyone in Clover Cove.'

Ryan shook his head. 'The moment this is all decided, I'll be on the first bus out of here.'

Connor started. 'What? Since when?'

'Since always brother. Got itchy feet, you know that. And all this?' he indicated the walls and ceiling. 'This is all yours.'

'Oh no Ryan, it's every bit as much yours as it is mine. Especially the kitchen, this is your domain.'

Ryan pulled a skeptical face. 'Then why did Mam put the deeds in your name?'

Connor sighed.

'Ry, we've been through this.'

'Have we?'

'It doesn't matter about what's on that piece of paper, it's your place as much as it is mine, you know that.'

'Well last time I looked, it said 'Connor's' above the door.'

'Yes, but Mam dumped it on me, I wasn't consulted! What am I supposed to do?'

'How should I know, I'm only the kid brother, right? No one tells me anything.'

Connor tightened his jaw. It was an old argument and one that never had a winner. Just before their father's funeral, Rose James had gathered the children in the bar and announced that she intended to leave for America to stay with her sister, Auntie Clare. Connor, she said, would take over running the pub. Rose had dropped it like an anvil, no discussions, no comebacks. And it had fractured an already splintering family.

'You know why Mam did it, Ry,' said Connor. 'Because she wanted to keep me in this bloody place. She knew that without it, I'd have left the moment Da's casket was in the ground.'

Ryan snorted.

'That's your story, is it?'

'Jesus, Ryan! Don't you remember what was on the walls of our bedroom growing up?'

Ryan didn't respond. *Stubborn, just like Mam.*

'Alright I'll say it: there were maps all over the walls. And postcards, pictures of beaches and mountains. And the bookshelves: full of what? Hemingway, Shackleton, John Buchan. I wanted adventure, I wanted to see the world. And Mam trapped me in this... this...'

'Goldmine?'

Connor gaped at him.

'You really think that?' He crossed to a bookshelf and pulled out a fat ledger. 'Here,' he said, dropping it onto the table with a thud. 'The cashbook. Be my guest, see the riches this place generates.'

Ryan didn't move, so Connor jabbed a finger down at the bottom of a page. 'See that? The final figure is in brackets. Do you know what that means? It means it's a negative number, Ryan. It means we owe the bank money we don't have. And not just the bank. The breweries, Bryan Carroll yesterday, the dairy this morning. I'm struggling to even pay Grace.'

'Okay, so we've had a few bad months...'

'Try a few bad years, Ryan. This place has been in debt since Da died.'

'But none of that matters now, does it? Ross Oil are

going to buy up the bar and you can fly off to fight bulls in Spain like Hemingway if you like.'

'What makes you think they're going to buy Connor's?'

'Why not? It's right in the center of the village.'

'Ry, clue yerself up. This isn't about real estate, it's a PR exercise. Ross have had a bellyful of bad publicity about the oil so now they're trying to change their image: "Look we're eco-friendly and fair trade" – it's all about polishing their halo, so the last thing they'd buy is a bar.'

Ryan crossed his arms: always a bad sign. It meant he wasn't going to budge an inch. He really was like their mother.

'Just because you've given up on life Con, doesn't mean I have. I still want to go out there and do things, see things. Why are you trying to stop me?'

'I'm not!' He shouted, then pulled himself up. Taking a deep breath, he said. 'Look Ryan, I'd love you to go and do everything I never could, I really would. But even if I thought Ross Oil would give us a million Euro for the bar, I'm not going to tell everyone in Clover Cove to abandon ship just because it's good for us.'

'Because you're still trying to make up for Da.'

'Make up for?' snapped Connor, his eyes wide. 'Make up for what? Do you blame me for what happened to him?'

Ryan glared at Connor, his face a mask of surliness. Finally, his head gave a little shake and he looked away. 'No. That was nobody's fault, but you *are* trying to be him, aren't you? Trying to be the head of the whole village.'

'I'm just trying to stop Mikey from blowing all his money on a gold-plated snooker table.'

There was a pause, then Ryan burst out laughing. Connor joined in, clapping his brother on the shoulder.

'Listen Ryan, I get you want to see the rivers and the

mountains, I really do. But you do know I'd rather you stayed here with me, don't you?'

Ryan looked him in the eye.

'And you know I'd rather you came with me, don't you?'

Connor nodded with a sad smile.

'Maybe. We'll see what happens, eh? Maybe Ross Oil will want to turn Clover Cove into the new Disneyland.'

'Well, I get to be Mickey.'

'What does that make me?'

'You, brother, are Goofy.'

Chapter 15

Kate walked towards Sleagh Castle, trying to get Connor James out of her mind. He was arrogant, self-centered, short-sighted and everything she hated in a man. Oh, and he had walked in on her when she was *in the tub!* What kind of throwback did something like that? And another thing: why was he so hostile towards her? All Kate had done was come here to do her job, to ask the residents of Clover Cove if they wanted a little money, possibly jobs, certainly improvements to their roads and infrastructure. She wasn't twisting anyone's arms, wasn't forcing it on anyone. She was just asking the question. And yet from the moment Kate had fallen through the door of Connor's, he had treated her like the devil herself.

Well perhaps Sir Charles Balcon would be more reasonable, she thought as she crossed the rest of the field. He could hardly be any more pig-headed.

Kate came to what appeared to be the edge of Balcon estate, a half-collapsed dry stone wall which looked as if a giant had given it a petulant shove, then left it lying on the hillside to gather moss and seagull poop. A rather forlorn wrought iron gate still stood however, next to a sign reading 'Keep OUT. No Access. No public Right Of Way. Trespassers WILL be prosecuted.'

'Hmm. Friendly too,' said Kate, unlatching the gate and wincing as it creaked on its hinges. Maybe the noise was an early warning system to detect anyone brave enough to defy the sign, thought Kate, scanning the grounds ahead for guard-dogs or a gamekeeper wielding a shotgun. But there was nothing except a muddy path that squelched under her boots, leading diagonally across a field towards the castle. She could see now that the building was older and far more grand than she had expected. The first thing that caught the attention was of course the castle's tower, a looming grey stone pillar with arrow-slit windows and Disney-style ramparts at the top. Clearly it was built as a fortress, to repel Viking or pirates or whatever other perils used to trouble this part of the coast, but over the centuries, other parts had been added to the castle; it had grown into a palace. Kate had always loved history and knew a little about the various styles of architecture: the main house to the side of the old castle had high arched windows and pointed gables with fussy carving around the edges, which would make it some sub-set of Gothic, meaning it had probably been built in the seventeenth century. In Ireland, of course, that was practically a new-build, but Kate could feel her excitement rising, entranced by the history. What stories did these walls hold? What had they seen? What love affairs and joys and tragedies? What wars and celebrations? The path finally joined a walkway of hard-packed stone, itself probably centuries old, which led towards the front of the house. Kate resisted the urge to peek in through the mullioned windows as she passed; she didn't want the owner to see her nose pressed up against the glass. Not a great first impression to make.

Instead, she skirted around the stone walls until she came to the large oak double doors with an iron bell-pull to the right. Kate reached up and, after a moment's hesitation, gave the handle a tug. It didn't move. She tried again, harder and the handle gave a rasping groan, moved two inches and stopped. Kate listened: no ring, no footsteps. She was just about to knock on the door when there as a roar behind her; a bright red sports car sped up the driveway and skidded to a halt, sending up a spray of gravel.

'Wouldn't bother with the bell,' said the driver, climbing out. 'Thing hasn't worked since the Boer War.'

He was tall and blonde, devilishly handsome, almost a negative of Connor James, Kate thought. Where Connor was dark and brooding, black hair falling across his brow, this man had neat golden hair and the cheekbones of a catwalk model. And his eyes – *heavens*, thought Kate. As blue as the sky.

'Charles Balcon,' he said, striding towards her, hand extended. 'You must be Katherine O'Riordan?'

Kate took his hand, warm and firm, feeling a prickle of electricity as she looked into those eyes.

'Yes, from Ross Oil,' she said, willing herself not to blush. 'I hope I'm not keeping you from anything?'

'Not at all, just been... running a few errands,' he said. 'As of now, I'm all yours.'

All mine? Thought Kate as Charles held her gaze for a second.

The man raised one eyebrow. 'Shall we?'

Kate opened her mouth, then realized she didn't know what she was going to say.

'Let me show you inside,' said Charles, gently touching Kate's arm and turning her towards the house. He twisted the big iron latch and threw the door wide. 'Never lock it,' he said, 'No point.'

Kate stepped into a huge open hallway. 'Wow,' she said. It looked like a Disney fantasy of a castle interior: a wide staircase lit from behind by grand latticed windows, wood paneling, oil paintings of medieval noblemen – there was even a suit of armor guarding the doorway to the left.

'Yes, it's quite the vision, isn't it?' said Charles, 'Every generation of Balcons has threatened to modernize, but no one seems to have got around to it.'

'I'm glad,' said Kate. 'It's spectacular.'

'Kind of you to say,' said Charles. 'To me, it's just... well, what home looks like, I suppose. If I changed it all to chrome and exposed brick, it would feel wrong. Mind you, we do have plenty of exposed brick already. Come through, come through.'

He led her through an open hallway to a grand sitting room at the back of the house, dominated by a carved marble fireplace big enough to walk inside. The bow windows gave a view of gardens rolling down to the cliffs, then beyond, the blue sea. *Blue like his eyes*, thought Kate, immediately reminding herself that she needed to be professional. This was a business meeting and an important one.

'Please, do sit down,' said Charles, indicating a pair of sofas facing each other over a polished wood table. 'If you'll excuse me for a moment, I'll see if I can rustle up some tea.'

As he disappeared, Kate took a moment to look around. The paintings, the furniture, the expensive-looking china and glassware... but it was the size of the room that was the most impressive. The ceilings were ridiculously high, carved with images of eagles and foxes, and right in the centre. a painted scene of cherubs and angels floating about.

'Funny, aren't they?' Charles was standing in the doorway holding a tray, following her gaze. 'I've always wondered what they were supposed to symbolize.'

'Remind us of our place in the heavens, perhaps?'

Charles laughed and s sat down on the sofa, crossing his legs. 'I see you're a poet, Miss O'Riordan.'

'Kate, please.'

He smiled that wicked smile again.

'Kate, of course. No, I rather fear that is quite the opposite of heavenly,' he said, looking up again. 'As I understand it, some of my ancestors were, shall we say, less than Godly. All manner of affairs and naughtiness. Apparently, there was a duel fought on the lawn outside over the honor of a lady.'

There was a roguish look of amusement on Charles Balcon's face that made Kate feel wrong-footed, as if he were challenging her, testing her to see how she reacted to stories of orgies and decadence.

'I, I came to discuss our project?' she said awkwardly.

'Of course, of course,' said Charles. 'Down to business. So what exactly is Ross Oil's interest in our little hamlet?'

He sat back and gazed at her, all polite curiosity, but Kate couldn't shake the feeling there was still a half-smile on his wide mouth.

'Well, right now nothing's decided, I'm really here to look at the possibilities. However, we are looking at an environmentally friendly energy-generating project, using the power of the sea.'

'Hmm, wave energy?' he said. 'Interesting. And what would you need from us?'

'Well, obviously, this would be a large-scale project. While we would strive to limit the impact on the environment, there would have to be building work. The energy-generating equipment in the sea, plus whatever shore-based structures are needed. And obviously, we would need access both inland and via the cove itself.'

'So you would need access through my land?'

'Again, I'm not entirely sure at this stage, but that seems

likely, given that you own most of the land south of the cove.'

Sir Charles nodded, pursing his lips. 'Intriguing,' he said, 'Very intriguing.'

Kate watched his face, hoping for some sort of reaction, but instead Charles jumped up. 'Well,' he said, 'clearly we need to discuss this in more depth.'

'Yes, of course,' said Kate.

'Splendid. Then I shall take you for lunch.'

'Oh, I'm not sure that is necessary.'

'Nonsense,' smiled Charles, throwing out a hand for Kate to take. 'The old place has its charms I suppose, but it looks like turning into a lovely day – we don't want to be cooped up, do we?'

'No, I suppose not...' stuttered Kate, allowing herself to be let back through the hallway and out through the front door.

'Besides, I doubt you had a chance to see exactly what we're discussing yet. We'll take the Coast Road – you can see what Ross Oil's money will buy.'

Before she could object, Charles had ushered Kate into his little sports car. The dashboard was polished walnut, the seats tan leather, it was sleek and low-slung. *Rather like its owner*, thought Kate as he fired the engine and took off in a shower of gravel.

The journey was mercifully short as Kate wavered between being transfixed by the beauty of the coastline and fearing for her life as Charles threw the powerful car around tight bends and down into valleys, braking only at the last minute. It was with some relief then when they finally he pulled up in front of a large white cottage standing alone on an isolated headland, views of the plunging coastline either side.

'Welcome to the Watch House,' said Charles, scooting

around the car's ticking engine to open Kate's door. 'As the name suggests, it was a coastguard cottage years ago, now it's the only restaurant in the area with a Michelin star.'

'Really? I was only expecting a sandwich.'

Kate was suddenly very aware that she was still wearing the wellington boots she had borrowed from the pub, but Sir Charles seemed to sense it.

'Don't worry, the chef Maurice is a friend of mine and I can assure you he doesn't insist on customers dressing for dinner. Plus he will do a cheese sandwich if that's what you fancy. But rest assured it will be the best cheese sandwich you've ever tasted.'

He held the door for her and Kate stepped into a minimal but cozy interior, all dark beams and scrubbed floorboards, an open fire in the centre of the room. Any fears of pretentiousness were immediately dispelled as Charles was embraced by a stocky man with an infectious grin, both of them laughing at some unheard joke.

'Katherine O'Riordan, may I introduce Maurice Bernard? Maurice is the greatest chef in Europe and Katherine is here to buy Clover Cove for her evil Yankee paymasters.'

'Well, I for one welcome our American friends,' said the Frenchman with a twinkle, 'We gave you the Statue of Liberty, it's about time you gave us something in return.'

Charles chuckled.

'What Maurice means is that more oil workers means more demand for his famous onion soup.'

'Bien sur,' said Maurice will a Gallic shrug, 'I am an artist and all artists want an audience, no? I cook my soup for Claudette, but she sneers and walks out.'

Charles raised an eyebrow. 'Don't worry, Claudette is the restaurant's resident cat. I'm sure she would prefer the fish pie.'

'No, she does not like my fish either. I think she prefers mice.'

Maurice showed them to a table right up against a picture window, giving an uninterrupted view of the coves and inlets all the way north. Now the rain had gone, Kate could just make out the white sugar cube of the chapel perched on the clifftop at Clover Cove.

'For the beautiful lady, I bring you wine on the house,' said Maurice, pushing Kate's seat in. 'The English m'Lord will have to buy his own.'

Kate briefly considered asking for water, but bit her tongue. She didn't think a gourmand Frenchman would take it too well.

'And shall I bring la carte?'

'Well if Kate has no objections, how about you bring us the soup followed by the fish pie?' Charles lent over and touched Kate's knee. 'I promise, your taste buds will thank me.'

'Soup and the pie it is,' said Kate, and Maurice went away happy.

'Does he really have a cat?'

'Oh yes, he's devoted to her. Although I'm not sure Claudette is quite so enamored. I have a suspicion that she's getting fed at the farm across the meadow.'

Charles was right about the soup: it was sublime. Kate wasn't sure if she'd ever had soup so good. Silky smooth and topped with perfectly grilled cheese that stuck pleasingly to the spoon, it was the right balance between sweet and savory. And Charles Balcon was sparkling company: amusing, polite but attentive. She couldn't understand why broody Connor James had warned her about Sir Charles. She had been expecting a leering septuagenarian with wandering hands. Perhaps it was a territorial thing.

'So you're English?' asked Kate.

Charles shook his head. 'Half and half. Mother Irish, Father from a grand English dynasty; I have stacks of cousins over there. But I was born here in that very house in fact,' he said, nodding towards the castle whose towers and chimneys were just visible through the window. 'But I was shipped off to English private school at seven to learn the manners of the Empire. I'm not entirely sure it worked, but after Cambridge and a spell in the Irish Guards, I came back here to take over running the estate. Papa was gone by then and my mother was barely hanging on.'

'I'm sorry,' said Kate.

'Oh, ancient history now. Point is, the locals all still think of me as 'the English Lord', despite the fact my passport is Irish and mother's family have lived here since William the Conqueror. I can't really blame them, centuries of having to doff their caps to the Laird and all that, but for me? This is home, always has been and I'm as passionate about the place as anyone.'

Kate thought of Connor James and his angry words last night.

'Does that mean you're for or against Ross Oil?'

Charles smiled.

'Let's talk money.'

Ah. Of course. That's what – usually – it came down to. How much and how soon.

'Well, broadly we have two options as I see it,' said Kate. 'We can buy a section of your land or we can pay you for access across it and permission to build on or under it – running cables, access roads and so on.'

Kate had spent long hours in the logistics department back in Manhattan, studying maps and sea tables and satellite images, looking at rainfall and tide variations and the mineral make-up of the land. There were always surprises when you actually began digging holes, but she guessed she knew far more about Charles Balcon's land than he did.

'So how much are we looking at?'

Kate recognized that look in his eye: greed. She had seen it in every negotiation she had ever been involved with.

'Well, if we're going to purchase the land, we would certainly pay market value with a sweetener on top, it would be very appealing, if I can put it that way.'

'Thousands, millions?'

Kate spread her hands. There was no point in being coy. David had made it clear they were in a hurry to get the project underway and Ross Oil had deep pockets. She pulled a pen from her pocket and wrote a figure on a napkin, folded it and pushed it across to him.

'I think you'll find that more than generous,' said Kate. 'It's in our interest that everyone is happy about the deal.'

Charles looked down at it, his mouth immediately pressing downward.

'Not enough?'

'Certainly not enough for what you're asking of Clover Cove. And of me, frankly. I do value the life I have here as much as any villager.'

Kate frowned. The offer was more than the land was worth; frankly she had expected him to bite her hand off. 'Then how much? It's in our interest that everyone involved is happy with the deal.'

'Happy,' he repeated. 'Interesting word. How much money do you think would make me happy?'

It was a strange question, but Kate had seen the Balcon family home, seen the cracks in the masonry and picked her way through the muddy, untended gardens. Yes, he had a shiny sports car, but it didn't look as if Charles Balcon was thriving financially. He could do with the money, that much was clear.

'It's not the first time I've been asked that question, Sir Charles,' said Kate. 'If you'd like an honest answer, then I don't think money has the power to make anyone happy, not really. Money in itself doesn't solve everything, but it's better than no money.'

'Well now, that depends on what you're really planning,' he said, his eyes straying out to the view.

'What we're *really* planning? Are you suggesting I'm not playing fair?' Kate kept her tone playful, but underneath, Kate was annoyed.

'I don't mean to cast aspersions on you, Kate, but this is Ireland. You'll find the people here have very long memories.'

'Meaning what?' said Kate, although she was thinking of the reaction to her grandpa's name in the bus on the way to Clover Cove. Clearly Charles was right about people bearing a grudge.

'Meaning this isn't the first time we've had foreign invaders coming to make a land-grab,' said Charles. 'The Vikings, the French, the English. Aristocratic farmers, mining corporations, the fishing industry, each bringing promises of making everyone rich and important. And yes, they come and take, but they leave us with less than when we began.'

'And your family...?'

'Correct, our house was built on the profits of farming hundreds of years ago, I can't deny that. The difference is that the Balcons stayed on and – I like to think – did something to add stability to the community. Call us guardians or caretakers if you like, and despite what certain people in the area think, I do take that role very seriously.'

'Well I can certainly assure you Sir Charles that Ross Oil has only good intentions for Clover Cove.'

Charles raised his glass. 'The road to hell is paved with good intentions.'

'And what does that mean?' said Kate, bristling.

'Calm yourself Katherine,' said Charles holding up a hand. 'I'm not questioning your integrity. The question is whether your intentions match up with your boss's intentions and *his* boss's intentions. We're in a global economy now Kate and what happens here doesn't happen in isolation.'

'I don't quite see...'

'Okay, so everything goes smoothly here. You build your wave technology, you're pumping clean electricity back into the community and the Irish economy. But then a Ross Oil tanker runs aground in the Philippines or America gets a new president who decides to slap a huge new tax on energy. Then what happens to Clover Cove? We both know Eco-Energy is the least profitable arm of your business, so Ross Oil pulls out, leaving us stranded.'

'You're right, Sir Charles, I can't guarantee any of those things won't happen. But I can tell you that as of today, Ross Oil intends to build something positive here, which will bring prosperity to the area.'

He fixed her with a stern look, his blue eyes locked onto hers.

'Do *you* trust Ross Oil, Kate?'

'I... I don't know.'

She looked down at the coast, perfect and pretty, bathed in bright sunshine. And she thought of David sitting behind his desk in Manhattan.

'No, actually, I don't trust them either,' she said honestly. 'Because you're right, there are hundreds of variables I have no control over and if push comes to shove, Ross Oil will do what's best for the shareholders of Ross Oil. But I can promise you *I* will do my best.'

Charles' stony face broke into a grin and he reached over and grasped Kate's hand.

'Congratulations, Miss O'Riordan. That was the correct answer.'

'So you'll work with us?'

'No.'

She gaped at him. 'But you just said...'

'If I was selling my land to Kate O'Riordan, I would have already signed the contract. You, Kate, I trust. But Mr. Ross Oil? He's a shark. And I won't risk all this.'

'But these people need us,' said Kate, feeling it all slipping away. 'You say you're a guardian or a caretaker, then take care of them. They're barely managing. Ross Oil will bring jobs and money and infrastructure.'

'You're right, there are plenty of families who'd take the money and dance a jig as their cottage was bulldozed. But then what will they do? Move to Galway where houses cost four times as much? Buy a satellite TV and a year's worth of Guinness? And then what?'

'That's their choice, Charles!' she snapped. 'You can't make decisions about people's lives.'

'Actually, I can,' he said, dabbing his mouth with a napkin and carefully placing it next to his plate. 'That's the joy and the burden of being a custodian. I can decide what's best for people, whether they agree with me or not.'

'That's so... You're just so...'

'Arrogant? Is that what you were going to say? Perhaps so, Kate. But I have to believe I'm right.'

'And what if you're wrong? Clover Cove isn't the only place on the west coast of Ireland blessed with waves, Sir Charles. All that money will simply go to another county, another village.'

'Then good luck to them.' He tapped the napkin Kate

had written her offer on. 'But this is not nearly enough to buy Clover Cove.'

'Okay, so you reject our money. What do you think's going to happen to those people out there?' she asked, gesturing towards the village.

'I think they'll have a community and family and a home to be proud of.'

'A home with a leaky roof and nothing on the kitchen table.'

'Perhaps, but when they open their curtains in the morning, they'll have the most beautiful view in Ireland.'

Kate stood up and snatched the napkin from the table.

'You can't eat a view, Sir. Charles.'

Kate was silent all the way back to the village, partly because she was angry with Charles, and partly because she was embarrassed. Dramatically stalking out of the restaurant lost some of its impact when she realized that she was stuck in the middle of nowhere. To his credit, Sir Charles simply followed her to the car and opened the passenger door. He didn't force conversation as he drove her back to the village.

Finally, they pulled up outside the pub just as Connor James was stepping out of the door. She watched his reaction as he saw Charles Balcon's car, saw the driver next to her. It was like a nature film she had once seen about rutting stags. His eyes seemed to bulge and turn yellow. If there hadn't been a windshield between them, Kate swore they would have lowered their antlers and started butting heads. With a final glare, Connor turned back into the pub.

It was only then that Sir Charles spoke.

'You're right,' he said.

'Right? About what?'

He looked at Kate with those piercing eyes.

'Perhaps I have been too arrogant.'

'Oh, um, good. Does this mean you'll change your mind?'

'Speak to your paymasters, bring me a sensible offer and I will consider it. But I have two conditions.'

'Two?'

'One, that the people of Clover Cove agree to a sale. If they decide it is a good thing for them and for the village, I won't stand in your way.'

'And the second condition?'

'That you have dinner with me.'

Kate's heart flipped.

'Charles, I don't think...'

'Non-negotiable I'm afraid. Think of it as a business meeting; your chance to pitch the Ross vision to me again.'

'Done,' she said and turned to open the door, but Charles placed a warm hand over hers.

'But Kate?'

'Yes.'

'Stay away from Connor James. He's trouble.'

Funny, he said the same thing about you, thought Kate.

Chapter 16

Charles Balcon. Sir Charles the snake, the rat, the vampire. Connor squeezed his hands into fists and tried to breathe. *It's your fault, you idiot,* he reminded himself. *You literally took Kate O'Riordan to him.*

He bumped a fist against his head.

So what? What's the girl to you? Why are you so mad about it?

Why? Because it was so typical that he would drive her back in his flash car, turning the girl's head with his money and his smooth ways. As he always did. Connor stomped through the bar, ignoring the calls of the various patrons already filling the bar, and pushed through the kitchen, grabbing his coat and heading for the back door. Up the path, turn left, then right and he was on a little secret pathway running behind the houses.

Shouting out in frustration, he kicked at a tree root and was rewarded with a sharp pain in his shin.

'You fool, Connor James,' he groaned, rubbing his leg. He looked up and down the lane, embarrassed at his own petulance. No-one was watching, not even the crows. He turned right and limped on. The secret path wasn't secret of course: everyone in the Cove knew it was there, but he had always thought of it as secret since he had been a small boy playing there on his own, imagining it as a smuggler's path or a war-torn trench or a haunted corridor, depending on where his imagination was taking him that day. 'Your head's always in the clouds, Connor James,' his father used to sigh. 'No good ever came of dreaming, boy.'

But Connor had disagreed, finding adventure and mystery in every corner, along every muddy path. Knights, pirates, fairies and dragons, you only had to open your eyes and see them. That had been then of course, when he'd been small. Of late, Connor had begun to think perhaps his father had been right. Why dream of monsters and witches and intrigue and betrayal when all those things were there to see, right under your nose?

He stopped at a rusted old gate, beyond it the old graveyard next to the church. The locals may well have known about the narrow path, but that didn't mean they ever used it. Connor knew full well that it had been twenty years since anyone had oiled the hinges of the gate, so he swung up onto the steps to the side: the stile, which made him think of Kate O'Riordan. Again.

Why am I so bothered by all this? He wondered. Not just Kate, but Ross Oil and the money and the chance of things changing.

'Why? Because it's home,' he whispered.

His little brother Ryan had been right of course, it wasn't up to Connor James what happened to the Cove. The residents of the village were all adults, they could and would make their own decisions, whatever the landlord of the Spa and Suites thought. And so what if everyone left? New people would come in to the empty cottages and stores; those which Ross Oil saw fit to leave standing of course. And they'd always need the pub. If he could afford to keep it running.

Perhaps that was what this was all about. The pub wasn't exactly on its last legs, but it wasn't far off. The tourism boosted by the power of social media he'd mentioned to Ryan had so far failed to materialize: the Cove was just too far off the beaten track. The American and Japanese coachloads with their cameras, dollars and yen all went to Killarney or the Cliffs of Moher for their fix of sweeping green coast and crashing waves.

Or maybe it *was* the girl, not Charles Balcon at all. Something about her and her red hair and her green eyes had got under his skin. The way she held her head in that defiant way, maybe it reminded him of his mother. Maybe.

And maybe something about her had stirred something in him that had been lying hidden since Ciara had run off with Charles Balcon.

Now *that* was why he had a half-broken toe. Connor pushed past an overgrown holly bush, then wove through the gravestones, most of them leaning or covered with moss. Very few people had been buried in the churchyard since about the nineteenth century, when a boom in the fishing industry had required a larger cemetery to be built on the road out of town, but you could just read some of the weathered inscriptions, many in Gaelic. As a youngster, Connor's father had often made him roll his eyes when he would hold forth about the importance of knowing your history, pointing out the meanings of the names of local village s or the root of modern Irish surnames. Connor spotted 'O'Cinnéide,' the Gaelic version of 'Kennedy', which his dad had taken great pleasure in pointing out translated as 'helmet-headed' and 'Mac Conmara,' the equivalent of the modern MacNamara, meaning 'hound of the sea.' Connor could almost see his father sitting at the end of the bar saying 'See,

Con? Be proud: we're all descended from the mighty Irish warriors who threw the Vikings back into the sea.'

And just like history, here came another foreign invasion, and like those ancient residents of the Cove, Connor was heading to the church for sanctuary and guidance.

A smile came to his lips as he knocked on the back door of the rectory. *Guidance*, he thought. *I must be desperate if I'm choosing the Declan as my advisor.* But then Connor and Father Declan had a different relationship to most in the village; they were friends, real friends. After Ryan, Declan was Connor's closest pal. The door opened and Connor was just about to bark out a greeting when he stopped. It wasn't Father Declan, but the lined, scowling face of an older man. Bishop Ray. The smile faded from Connor's face.

'Ah, it's yourself Connor James,' said the old priest, 'And what would the likes of you be doing here? Come to sell us some of your whiskey?'

Connor forced a smile. Bishop Ray had never made any secret that he disliked Connor or his family. Connor's father had had a number of run-ins with the priest when he'd been plain Reverend Ray and the vicar here before Declan. Hard-line in every way, Ray was against 'the drink,' encouraging his congregation to boycott bars selling alcohol; always a difficult task in Ireland where the pub is an important part of the social fabric. Connor's dad Cormac had faced Ray down, pointing out that he had been providing communion wine free of charge for years, but the antipathy only got worse when Ray was promoted to Bishop.

'No whiskey today,' said Connor. 'Just here to see Father Declan.'

'*Reverend* Declan, you mean?' said the old man, his mouth pursing in disapproval.

'Yes, that's him. Is he in?'

Connor heard his friend's voice coming from inside.

'Ah Connor, do come in.'

There was a heavy pause before Bishop Ray reluctantly stepped aside. *Just like the post office,* thought Connor with a hidden smile. The old priest's campaign of saving the lost souls of Ireland had come to an abrupt halt ten years ago when he had tried to blockade the Post Office in the square. His beef had been that the Post Office sold both cigarettes and 'titillating' magazines such as the TV Guide. However, the busy-body spinsters who had willingly supported his campaigns against drunkenness and fornication had drawn the line at being denied access to the local gossip that was habitually exchanged in the Post Office, and Father Ray found himself alone on the picket line. That was when Ray had been 'kicked upstairs to save face,' as Connor's Dad had put it.

'Good to see you, Con,' said Declan, shaking his hand formally. 'I dare say you've come to discuss the catering for the village fair?'

He widened his eyes meaningfully.

'Oh yes,' said Connor, glancing towards the Bishop whose flinty eyes were watching him closely. 'That's right. Thought we should talk about the sausages and so on.'

'Not about the girl from Ross Oil, then?' said Ray. 'It's just it seems that's all anyone's been talking about for the last few days.'

Connor felt the old man's eyes on him, waiting for a response.

'Sure, there has been some discussion in the bar,' he said reluctantly. 'But I guess we'll have to wait and see, won't we? The girl – Miss O'Riordan, that's her name – says she's only here on a fact-finding mission right now.'

'And that'll be why she was discussing money with Sir

Charles over lunch, will it?' said Ray. That got Connor's attention.

'Money? What have you heard?' he said looking from Ray to Declan and back again.

Bishop Ray smiled the thin smile of one who enjoys withholding information.

'Alex, the waiter from the Watch House? He rang a few minutes ago,' said Declan quickly. 'All we know is that figures were discussed. Big numbers.'

'So we know that there's going to be some changes around here, don't we Connor m'boy?' said the Bishop with some relish, then bent to pick up his coat. 'Well, I'll leave you boys to discuss the hot dogs, shall I?'

Declan gestured to Connor that he should wait while he showed the old man out. When he returned, he had a pained look on his face.

'Sorry Con, you know what Bishop Ray's like.'

'They don't call him "Ray of Sunshine" for nothing. He does seem to be relishing the idea of having the Cove bull-dozed into the sea.'

'Oh, he's not that bad, Con.'

'Isn't he?'

'Actually he's as worried as the rest of us. It's just...well, the history with your family and all.'

Connor nodded glumly and waved a hand. It was old news and they had more pressing matters to discuss. He sat down at the kitchen table.

'So what do you make of this Ross woman, Dec?'

Declan smiled and turned to fill the kettle.

'Are you asking about the potential oil investment or about the pretty girl with the red hair?'

'What? No!' spluttered Connor, 'I'm just worried about the village.'

'Sure,' said Declan.

Connor looked at him, not sure if he was being teased. He and Declan had been friends ever since the priest had come to the village; they had the same sense of humor and a shared love of nature, plus it had been a relief for Connor to find somebody in the village he could confide in without it being reported straight back to Orla at the post office.

'Look, I'm not completely dead, I know the girl is...'

'Beautiful?'

'Passable. But that doesn't change the fact that she is about to do something that could destroy this village.'

Declan was quiet for a moment as he busied himself making the tea. He brought two mugs over and sat down across the table from Connor. 'Look, first of all I don't think that is her intention. From the short time I spent with her, I got the feeling that she was pretty genuine.'

'Maybe, but Ross Oil is a huge conglomerate, they're used to getting what they want, no matter what one employee might say, so I think we need to organize as soon as possible...'

Declan held up a hand.

'That's the second thing, Con. You don't have to take it all on your own shoulders. I know that is what your dad used to do, your mum too I hear, but it's not hereditary. I know people look to you for advice, you don't have to feel that it's all your responsibility.'

Connor wanted to argue, but he knew his friend was right.

'It's just...'

'What?'

'It's just I seem to be the only one talking any sense here. Everyone seems to be counting all this phantom gold, buying Lear Jets and private islands, when I have this nightmare about Clover Cove falling into the sea.'

'Funny, isn't it?'

Connor looked up, raising an eyebrow.

'Me, you mean? The teenage rebel being the responsible one.'

Declan smirked. 'I have heard the stories.'

'Don't believe all you hear.'

'That's the strange thing, Con. I never hear anything bad about you. "Ah, he was a scamp, but he was good to his Ma," that sort of thing.'

Connor looked down at this mug.

'Yeah well, it's easy to be a rebel when you have this ironclad conviction that your parents are always going to be there holding everything together, doing the right thing while you kick against it.'

'And now you feel you're the one who has to do the right thing?'

'Yes, I guess.'

'You're right Connor, you do,' said Declan, 'But you only have to do the right thing for *you*, not the rest of the village.'

Connor looked at him in surprise.

'I'd have thought you of all people want to keep this community together.'

Declan shook his head. 'As a priest, my responsibility is to the souls of the community, not the bricks and mortar. And yes, I want them to make the right choices, but according to their own consciences. And that includes you, Con. No one should be doing anything that makes them unhappy.'

'Why do you say that? What makes you think I'm unhappy?'

He looked at Connor meaningfully.

'What do you really want, Con? Do you really want to hold it all together for everyone else? Are you convinced that's the right way to go?'

'I wish I knew, Father.'

Declan laughed.

'You only call me 'Father' when you're trying to avoid the question.'

Connor finished his tea and stood up.

'Yeah, well maybe that's what I'm trying to do.'

'At the risk of sounding like an American chat show, you need to follow your heart, Con. It sounds cheesy, but it's really the only path when it comes to big decisions – and affairs of the heart.'

'And what's that supposed to mean?'

Declan grinned and clapped his friend on the shoulder. 'You figure it out. You're the one with all the answers.'

'I wish I was, Father. I wish I was.'

Chapter 17

Kate walked down towards the sea, her pace brisk, her mood determined. Passing the houses and little shops, she came to the harbor and walked out along the harbor wall. The tide was in now and the waves were slapping gently against the bricks. She pulled out her phone and held it in the air: miracle upon miracle – a signal!

She clicked to texts and began to compose a message.

Villagers hostile, Charles Balcon greedy, considering pulling out.

Kate looked down at it, then shook her head and clicked off. *Calm yourself, Kate,* she thought, taking a deep breath of sea air. She closed her eyes and saw Connor James' face in her mind's eye. The look of distrust and anger she had seen flare when she had pulled up in Charles Balcon's sports car. The nerve of the man! And why was he angry with *her*? It had been Connor who had taken her to the man's house in the first place! Perhaps he expected her to storm out of the castle and refuse to talk to Charles? He was maddening!

And Charles Balcon wasn't much better. He was smooth and charming of course, but underneath? He pretended to care for Clover Cove and its residents, but really he was only interested in driving up the price. It always came down to money. Always.

Kate turned and looked back up towards the square, thinking professionally now. If Ross couldn't go across the Balcon land, then she needed to think about alternatives. But where would the cables go? It was too inefficient – and potentially too dangerous in a storm-swept cove – to run them overhead and the twisting nature of the road wasn't ideal to bury them, neither was the narrow space between some of the houses great for vehicular access: they'd definitely have to make room, which would mean moving walls, possibly knocking down whole houses. Some of the buildings close to the sea would have to go too, she thought. In order to have large ships docking, the jetty on which she stood would have to be extended and modernized, meaning two or three of the little cottages clustered down there would have to be demolished.

But none of that mattered if Kate couldn't persuade the villagers that it was in their interests to get behind the project. In fact, if even one of them dug their heels in, it could scupper the whole thing. Which was why it would be so much more simple to go through Sir Charles' land, but Kate was loath to give in to him.

She shook her head angrily. *Men.* Connor, Charles, even David: all just overgrown kids wanting their own way and bawling if they didn't get it.

Maybe it *was* all a waste of time, she thought. Perhaps she should look at one of the other possible sites up the coast. But that would mean admitting defeat after only two days and Kate was never a quitter. She had come here to do a job and she was determined to do it.

Sighing, she turned back to the phone and called up David's number. She needed to check in, give him an update, however bad it looked. The dial tone chirped once, twice – and Kate felt a wave of relief as it switched to voicemail.

'Hey David,' she said. 'Greetings from sunny Ireland.'

She pulled a face. Too breezy, too personal. She needed to keep it business-like.

'Just spoken to Charles Balcon, the landowner over here. Going through his estate would certainly be quickest and easiest. He wasn't against the project in principle, but he definitely senses an opportunity to take advantage. My feeling is that he will hold out for more money than we have in budget. So I'm going to "Plan B," looking to persuade the residents to sell up.'

There was a beep in her ear and Kate looked at the phone's screen and bit off a curse. Low battery. She hadn't plugged it in last night after speaking to Ginny.

'Gotta go. Will update you tomorrow. L...' She just stopped herself at the word 'love': force of habit. Whatever had possessed her to date her boss?

'Later...' she said lamely and clicked off.

Riiiiing. Rinnnnggg!

The phone immediately began ringing again. David? She thought with a lurch.

'Hello?'

'Honey, at last!' trilled Ginny. 'I've been trying to get hold of you for like, an age. How's Ireland? How are the men? Dark and handsome?'

Kate couldn't help laughing.

'Some are dark, some are blonde. And yes, some *are* handsome.'

'I knew it! So jealous. I never get to go anywhere.'

'Well, it's not all good news. Things aren't exactly going smoothly. I just left a message for David.'

'David? But it's over between you two, isn't it?'

'A business message, Gin. He's still my boss. And I don't think he's going to be very happy with me.'

'Don't let him push you around, hun,' said Ginny. 'Put your foot down, show him you don't need him anymore.'

Kate pulled a face.

'I'm not sure...'

'Well I am, Kate O'Riordan,' said Ginny. 'You're a strong...' – and then she stopped.

'Gin? You there?'

Kate looked down at the screen. Dead.

Just like this project, thought Kate. *Just like my love life.*

She pocketed the phone and walked back along the jetty, her eye drawn to the buildings nearest the water, suddenly curious over why anyone would build a house right on the seafront. Historically, this coastline was battered by storms in winter, that was why most of the cottages were clustered around the square, huddled together for protection. As she got closer, Kate quickly saw that the grey stone buildings weren't cottages at all, but commercial structures: presumably once used for fishing. The nearest to the harbor had large wooden doors leading onto a ramp; for storing or repairing boats perhaps and one had a high ceiling, used for drying or storing nets she guessed – although it had tall windows, which would be odd for a building facing the sea. Anyway, it didn't matter what they had been used for in the past, what mattered was who owned them now and whether they would be prepared to sell. Kate walked around the larger structure, cocking her head critically. Could it be adapted for modern use? It was large enough, certainly and Kate would much prefer to leave as much of the village as intact as possible. As she turned to the landward side, she noticed the painted board standing outside: 'Clamshell Gallery,' it read in swirly writing. 'Fáilte roimh chách.'

Kate couldn't believe she hadn't seen it on her walk earlier, but then perhaps the sign had been taken inside to prevent a gust taking it halfway down the beach.

She pushed the door and stepped inside. She had been right about the scale of the building. The roof was at least twenty feet high and there were tall windows with open shutters letting light flood in. And right in the centre of the room was an amazing sculpture of carved wood draped with twisted ropes like vines running up a tree.

'That's amazing,' said Kate.

'Do you really think so?'

Kate turned in surprise, both to see the woman in a paint-spattered shirt, but also at her English accent. The girl was late twenties at a guess, her blonde hair was pinned up, strands falling carelessly across her face, but she was still strikingly beautiful, like an off-duty model.

'I do have smaller pieces if you're interested,' said the woman, indicating a row of tables to Kate's left which were loaded with equally interesting creations. 'I like to work on the larger scale, but I know most people have, well, doors, which tend to get in the way.'

'Actually, I was thinking on an even bigger scale,' said Kate.

'Bigger?'

'I was wondering if you'd sell me your entire gallery.'

The woman paused, her mouth open, then threw her head back and laughed.

'Ah, you'll be the Ross Oil woman?' she put out a hand, looked at it, wiped it on her dungarees, then put it out again. 'Tessa Drake. I'm the local Bohemian.'

'Kate O'Riordan. Local pariah.'

Tessa laughed again.

'Charlie Balcon turned you down, I take it?'

'Yes, how did you...?'

The woman gave a knowing smile.

'Why don't you come through to the workshop, I'll make tea,' she said. 'If you're going to buy my studio, you'll want to see the whole place, won't you?'

Tessa walked past Kate and hung a sign on the door. 'Probably on the beach' it read. Kate followed her back through a doorway into a smaller room equipped with all manner of woodworking equipment. Chisels, saws, some sort of electric sander. To one side, there were a series of large painted canvases half-covered in sheets and at the back was a scarred work surface with a kettle already puffing steam like smoke signals.

'Have a seat,' said Tessa. 'You're probably sick of the sight of tea by now, but it's all part of the process here, like smoking a pipe of peace.'

Tessa brought over two mismatched mugs and an open packet of biscuits.

'So how is it that everyone in Clover Cove seems to know my business better than I do?'

Tessa smiled and picked up a biscuit.

'Kate, I'm an outsider too: I've only been here a couple of years, but I've learnt the hard way how it works. You've seen the village; it's not exactly over-run with cinemas and bowling alleys, is it? So when there's so little to do, gossip becomes the local pastime. You only have to think something and your neighbor will be running next door to pass it on, leading to Chinese whispers of course.'

'Chinese...what?'

'Chinese whispers. Maybe you called it something else in America? It's a child's game where one kid whispers something in another's ear, then that kid whispers it on to the next, usually making funny mistakes...'

'Ah yes, we called it "the Telephone game."'

'Right, same process, anyway. Mary says to Margaret

that the oil company is thinking of running a pipe through the village, by the time it's been passed through Joan, Jenny and John, the oil company is going to build a refinery in the middle of the square.'

Kate thought of the headline on the newspaper and how Molly in the cafe had known about the project before David had given her the go-ahead in his office.

'I think it's the same everywhere,' said Kate. 'Back in New York, the Ross Oil headquarters is on 30 floors, sometimes with six offices on each floor. You can imagine the rumors and counter rumors that fly about. So you're English too? Like Charles Balcon, I mean.'

'*Not* like Charles, I hope,' said Tessa. 'And as I'm sure he's told you, he's not actually English. No, I grew up in London and came out here to work, foolishly believing that it would be quieter.'

'It's not?'

Tessa laughed.

'You have surely noticed that the Irish like to talk?'

'I have,' she smiled. 'And I get that people have been talking, but how did you know Charles Balcon had turned me down? I only stepped out of his car about ten minutes ago.'

'Maurice the chef,' said Tessa. 'He told Dara in the kitchens who texted me. But I could have saved you the trip to the Watch House – Sir Charles was never going to agree to sell.'

'But doesn't he need the money?'

'Oh yes, the castle's mortgaged to the hilt, that flash sports car's on lease and he's living on hand-outs from his famous relatives.'

'Famous?'

'Well, famous in Europe anyway. His cousin Serena's an actress and her sister's a designer.'

'Gosh, *those* Balcons? I love Venetia Balcon's stuff; in fact, I have some of her shoes with me.'

'Well I wouldn't wear them on the beach if I were you.'

Kate laughed. She liked this girl, felt an affinity with her in the same way she and Ginny had clicked.

'So if Charles is struggling financially, why say no to Ross Oil?'

'Because for all his faults, Charlie Balcon has one thing he prizes above all else: history. He has something of a hang-up about how his family exploited the people.'

'Like, two hundred years ago?'

'More like four, but as you'll find in Ireland, four hundred years ago might as well have been four weeks ago when it comes to hanging onto the past.'

Tessa pushed the hair from her face.

'Anyway, now Charlie's trying his best to look after us. Or at least, that's what he thinks he's doing.'

'Isn't he?'

'I'm from the big city: I think modern people with internet connections should be allowed to make their own choices. But his heart's in the right place – most of the time, anyway.' She blushed and looked away.

Kate wanted to ask what that meant, but suspected it was a subject off limits. One to file away for later.

'Well, in his defense, Sir Charles did claim Clover Cove is the most beautiful place in the world.'

'And Sir Charles is welcome to his opinion, but Sir Charles has already been around the world and there are many who would like to make that call for themselves.'

Tessa tilted her head to one side, fixing Kate with a shrewd look.

'So is Ross Oil going to buy me out?'

'Well that depends,' said Kate, 'I'd hate to run you out, especially when this place is clearly inspiring you to make beautiful things. But even if I did, it would only make sense to buy this place if I could persuade everyone else to join in.'

Tessa shrugged.

'But without the Balcon estate, you don't have much choice. This harbor is the only deep water for miles north and unless you were thinking of dynamiting the cliffs – and the chapel – the lane down to the cove is the only way to run your cables. Or am I wrong?'

Kate looked at her in amazement. It had taken her and the logistics team over six months to come to that very conclusion.

'I'm impressed,' she said.

Tessa smiled. 'I spend a lot of time on the beach looking at the landscape. I probably know the shape of the headlands and bays better than most people.'

After reading the report, David had been all for recommending, as he put it, 'blowing the church', but thankfully their boss Leo took the view that that might not play well with the natives. But as Tessa had pointed out, using the harbor road meant that it would have to be dug up to lay the cables, which would mean huge upheaval not to mention cost.

And suddenly Kate realized that she had been outmaneuvered. Charles Balcon had pulled a clever double-bluff, like tossing a two-headed coin. In order to get him to agree to using the Balcon estate, she would have to persuade the villagers to take the Ross Oil gold and abandon their homes, some of them forever. But at that point, Kate would then have to turn around and say, 'sorry folks, I'm running the cables across the Balcon estate instead,' leaving the villagers feeling tricked and resentful towards Ross Oil. It would be like offering them a prize, then snatching it away to give to the wealthy landowner.

At which point Charles Balcon could either refuse the Ross deal to make a point, or triple the price as Kate would be left with no options.

'What's up?'

'I've just realized I've been tricked.'

'By a man?'

'Of course.'

'C'est la vie, Kate.'

Kate dropped her head to her chest and groaned. The only possible option now was to go through the village and up across the square – and make it work. Kate had a sinking feeling in her stomach, because that would require her to persuade dozens of people – including Connor James.

'You've lived here a few years, Tessa – how many people do you think might want to sell up?'

Tessa pursed her lips. 'I'll be honest with you Kate, as it stands, it's a coin flip.'

'Fifty-fifty?'

Tessa nodded.

'I think some heads have been turned by the idea of a windfall, and some are happy as they are and don't want change. All sorts of things at work: family, relationships, greed. A lot of greed.'

There was that word again.

'There's been a lot of giddy talk about what they're going to do with the money, like it's a lottery win. Cars and boats and holidays.'

'And the people who don't want to move?'

'Oh, they're excited too. As I say, nothing much happens in Clover Cove. But they're frightened by the prospect. And Ireland's not big on change generally; they value the past as much as the present.'

Kate gave a whistle.

'So how should I play it?'

'My advice? Treat it like the lottery. Tell everyone it's a big win for the community, new roads, a roof for the church, maybe even a cinema. That way even those sticklers who don't want to sell up will find it hard to resist.'

Kate nodded. It was generous advice, considering Tessa Drake seemed happy where she was.

'Thanks Tessa,' she said, standing. 'You've been a great help.'

'No problem. But be careful. Charles Balcon isn't the only player in town.'

'You mean Connor James?'

Tessa grinned.

'As I say, you be careful.'

As Kate stepped out of the gallery and walked back up to the square. On the far side, a group of middle-aged women were standing in a huddle next to Father Declan and elderly man in a dark overcoat. They all looked up with serious expressions and Kate had the distinct impression that they had just been talking about her, probably speculating on her every move. Lunch with Charles Balcon, a private audience in at Tessa's gallery: what can it all mean? In fact, Kate reminded herself that they all knew what it meant. Perhaps she should simply go up to each person and hand them a fistful of Euros. She remembered her dad taking her to buy her first car; on the way, he stopped at the bank to draw out a stack of cash in low-denomination bills. 'Wave real money under people's noses,' he'd said, 'They jump real quick'.

She heard a bark and Fiddle bounced across towards her, followed by Father Dec and the man in the overcoat. Kate patted the dog on the head.

'Looks like she's taken to you, Kate.'

'At least someone has.'

She saw Dec's companion was an older man also wearing priest's robes.

'Miss Katherine O'Riordan, may I present Bishop Raymond Lynch?' said Declan formally.

'Pleased to meet you, Bishop,' she said, wondering if she was supposed to curtsey. How did you curtsey, anyway? There wasn't a lot of call for it in Manhattan.

'Please to meet you too, Miss O'Riordan,' said the Bishop. 'And how are you finding the old country? I understand your grandfather is a native?'

'It's beautiful,' said Kate. 'And yes, my Gramps grew up near here.'

Bishop Ray nodded. 'Ah, young Gerry, I knew him well.'

Kate started.

'You know my granddad?'

'Oh yes, he was quite the character back in the day. I knew you were related the moment I saw you Katherine, you have his eyes. Not his temperament though, I hope.'

Kate laughed nervously. There was something in the way the old man was watching her, like a hungry vulture. She wanted to ask more about his memories of her grandfather, but she wasn't at all sure she would like what she heard. Some people just loved thinking the worst. And with that thought an idea popped into Kate's head. She looked across at the group of women, still whispering in a huddle, then back at Bishop Ray.

'Say Father,' she said, turning to Declan. 'Can I borrow your church tomorrow night?'

Chapter 18

Raff the fisherman looked at the clock above the bar, then down at his own watch, tapping a calloused finger against the glass.

'Not long until the meeting, Con,' he said. 'So are you going to close the pub?'

Connor finished pouring a pint of Guinness and set it in front of Raff.

'And why would I be doing that?'

He was aware that although the dozen or so drinkers in Connor's were engaged in their own conversations, they had one ear cocked so they didn't miss anything important. It was a skill children learned at an early age in Clover Cove, like sharks being able to sleep with one eye open.

'Why? Because at seven o'clock the bar's going to be empty,' answered Raff, draining half the beer. 'Everyone's going to finish their drinks and head over to the church to hear what Miss Kate's got to say.'

Connor picked up one of the flyers announcing the 'Public Meeting', which had been left all around the bar.

'Nice, aren't they?'

Connor looked at him. 'Your handiwork, Raff?'

The big man looked slightly abashed.

'Yes, well no. Miss Kate did it on her computer, she just asked me if I had a printer, so I steered her across to Orla at the Post Office. Oh, and I showed her how to use the photocopier: you know, it gets stuck unless you hold the button down? Anyway, I was only trying to help out. Being neighborly.'

Connor raised a sceptical eyebrow and read the handbill, printed in large bold letters.

Ross Oil Public Meeting

St. Augustine church, Clover Cove

Begins 7pm

Presentation regarding proposed Eco Energy Project

Followed by a chance to ask questions of Kate O'Riordan, Director of Development, Ross Oil

Buffet available

'Am I to assume that the buffet was your idea?'

'What makes you say that?' said Raff defensively.

'Because it's been scribbled at the bottom in your handwriting.'

'Oh. Well, the poor girl didn't know that you need to offer a sandwich. Local customs, you know.'

'And you'll be selling the sandwiches?'

Raff looked shocked.

'What are you, Sherlock Holmes?'

Connor smiled.

'There's butter in your hair, Raff.'

'Well, a man's got to make a living since the fish ran out.' He said, absently smoothing his unruly fringe.

'Anyway, to answer your question,' said Connor, 'The pub will stay open.'

'You're not coming?'

'No.'

Raff eyed him.

'And here was I, thinking you were dead against the Ross Oil people changing Clover Cove.'

Connor shook his head and addressed his answer to the bar.

'I've just been saying we should all take a breath and think things through properly before we all go off buying ping-pong tables and hot tubs.'

He looked meaningfully across at Mikey who suddenly found immense interest in his beer mat.

'Well I think you should go, brother.'

He turned; Ryan was leaning against the door. 'You go, I'll watch the bar, although Raff's right. I don't think anyone will be here: who's going to miss the big Lottery draw?'

Connor sighed and looked at Raff.

'Looks like I'll go then. But only because you make such fine sandwiches.'

Secretly Connor was glad to have an excuse to attend to the meeting. Ryan was right: it was the biggest thing to happen in the village since, well, since... he closed his eyes. He didn't want to think about that.

'Don't you want to go?'

Ryan shrugged.

'Sure, and I'll hear the whole thing replayed blow-by-blow for the rest of the night. Besides, yer man Raff's right, there will be no one in the bar. He nodded towards the television screen. 'I'll be watching the gaa.'

Ah. 'Gaa' was a local term for 'sport', in this case Gaelic football. Connor had been an enthusiast himself as a younger man, yelling himself hoarse in stands and bars. Just one more thing he'd given up since they wrote the word 'Connor's' over the door.

Connor left his brother in the bar and pushed through the back, just reaching for his coat as Kate O'Riordan came down the stairs.

'Ah Miss Kate,' he said. 'You'll be going to the church, will you?'

'I imagine you already know the answer to that, Mr. James,' she said. Her tone was brisk and Connor immediately felt his hackles rise. He was only going to offer to walk her across. He looked up at her.

'Have I done something to offend you?'

'And what could you have possibly done to offend me?'

'I'm sure I wouldn't know.'

She looked at him for a long moment.

'No, you probably wouldn't, would you?'

'Well perhaps you'd better enlighten me.'

She pursed her lips, as if she was considering what to say next.

'Is there a problem between you and Charles Balcon?'

Apart from being an arrogant pompous pretty boy? Apart from the Balcon family having lorded it over the entire county for generations? And apart from Charles Balcon having run off with the only woman Connor had ever loved?

'Nothing you need to know about,' said Connor.

'That's not an answer,' said Kate. 'Because this afternoon it looked to me like you both wanted to scratch each other's eyes out.'

'As I say, not anyone else's business.'

'But it is, Connor, if it affects what I'm doing here. If you are blocking the Ross Oil project because of some personal vendetta...'

'There is no vendetta, I assure you. I couldn't care less what Charles Balcon does with his money.'

Kate began to speak, but Connor put up a hand. 'What I *do* care about is making sure that people in Clover Cove make the right decision for Clover Cove and not just because they fancy having a bigger car.'

Connor began to pull on his coat.

'I'm coming to the meeting like everyone else, to see what you have to say, and I promise you, Kate O'Riordan, that I will come with an open mind.'

He smiled at her.

'Persuade me. Persuade us all. Answer all the questions we have and you won't have any problems. We're not the backwoods eejits you think.'

Connor slipped out the back door, before she could answer. He took his secret path up towards the church and through the trees, where he could see people already streaming in through the open doors. Organ music was coming from the inside: 'A Whiter Shade of Pale.' Connor gave a rueful smile. It was a wonder Dec wasn't ringing the bells to summon the entire parish. Connor stopped at the gate and checked his watch: just enough time. Turning away from the church, Connor took the left fork of the path which led away from the backs of the houses and up a steep track. It was even more overgrown up here, the bushes snagging and pulling at his sleeves, but finally it opened out to grass and heather. Connor turned and stood, his breath fogging in the cool evening air. From here he could see the whole village cloaked in darkness, an orange-yellow glow from lamp or fireside peeking from window-sockets here and there.

Clover Cove, he thought. So peaceful and unsuspecting. Was it about to change forever? Would those warm cottages even be there in a year's time? Would all those people he could just see walking up the church path be here next Christmas? He looked up as a gull gave a sharp cry in answer as it swooped high overhead, going back to her nest in the cliff behind him, blissfully unaware of the troubles of man far below.

'Maybe you're right, buddy,' he smiled softly. 'Maybe it isn't my business.'

What he had said to Kate O'Riordan had been true; what he had said to Ryan too. He had no desire to be his father. Cormac James had embodied Clover Cove, had been part of it down to his bones. He'd been a fisherman, a hill-walker and a singer of the old songs, he'd been connected to this land as much as if he was rooted like an oak. Whether he was manning the lifeboat or standing behind the bar, Cormac led the village in every way. Connor wasn't like that. He didn't have his father's unshakable certainty. He didn't have his wisdom. But he would do his best and – unlike his father sometimes – he would listen to what the people of the village wanted. That much he could do.

Connor turned his face towards the black empty space where the sea would be, the distant lights of Sleagh Castle to the left, the lantern over the door of the clifftop chapel to his right. *I wish you were still here, Da,* he thought, fighting the tugging in his chest. Lord knew, they had butted heads when Connor was a teenager, but Cormac James always seemed to know the right way to go. He was like a light-house steering the village into safe waters. *Steering me,* thought Connor.

Perhaps that was why his mother had been so adamant that Connor should stay in the Cove as landlord. With his father gone and she herself slipping away, the rock under the bar was the one solid thing she could offer him. And the truth was he *had* chosen this path. That was something he hadn't said to Ryan back in the kitchen. It was true their mother had willed the bar to him, but if he'd really wanted to, Connor could simply have sold the business and moved to Catalonia or Key West, chasing that boyhood dream of travel and swashbuckling adventure. But he'd stayed.

'Maybe I do like it here after all,' he said with a smile and turned back towards the church. 'And if Mikey wants a chocolate fountain, so be it.'

Chapter 19

Kate looked out over the sea of expectant faces all turned her way, fighting the nerves making her hands tremble in her lap. Molly from the café caught her eye and gave her an encouraging smile and she could see Charles Balcon sitting near the front talking to Orla from the post office: the whole village seemed to be here. This wasn't Kate's first time speaking in public of course; presentations were a part of the job. In the boardroom on the thirtieth floor, at conferences in front of bigwigs and politicians, she'd even occasionally spoken on Bloomberg and other business news programs, which had certainly pleased her mother if not David.

But this audience was unlike any other she'd faced. The pews were packed, Raff's buffet was doing a brisk trade and there was laughter and a warm rumble of chatter bouncing off the stone walls. The atmosphere was more like a Little League baseball game than a public meeting about the future of their village.

Kate tried to concentrate on the notes in front of her. Father Dec had set up a table in front of the altar and even found an artist's easel for Kate to display her hurriedly printed illustration boards. All of which just made Kate feel more exposed.

'Are we ready to go?' asked the priest, sidling up. 'It's just I've got a baptism first thing in the morning so I'll be needing to sweep up the sandwich crusts before I turn in...'

'Sure, no time like the present,' said Kate, forcing a smile.

Declan reached over to squeeze Kate's hand. 'If it's any help, I feel exactly the same before I give a sermon,' he whispered. 'I preferred going into a combat zone when I was in the army if I'm honest. I've heard it can help if you picture everyone naked.'

Kate looked towards the crowd, catching sight of Bishop Ray, his eyes hooded like an owl's. The expression on Kate's face must have conveyed her dismay because Declan leant in and added. 'No, it's never worked for me either.'

He gave her a brief thumbs-up, then stepped up to the pulpit and waited for the crowd to shush each other to quiet.

'Well it's grand to see so many people here tonight,' said Declan. 'You *do* know you're all also welcome to come on a Sunday, don't you?' That got him a laugh.

'So let's get to it: Miss O'Riordan has been good enough to come here and put her case, I'd ask you all to show as much respect. There will be time for questions at the end.' He looked meaningfully across the church. 'So no heckling, Mikey, eh?'

Another laugh and Father Dec stepped aside. Kate was surprised to get a ripple of applause as she stood up.

'Hello everyone,' she began, hoping they couldn't hear the wobble in her voice. 'Thanks for coming to hear what I have to say. I would like to begin by saying that Ross Oil is not the enemy. We are looking to site an energy project in the Cove, end of story. If everyone agrees it's a good idea – and I hope you will – then we'll build it. If not, then we'll find another site. We're not here to force anything on you. There would of course be some changes, but I believe they would certainly be balanced by the jobs and money that would come to the area. But overall my message tonight is this: it's up to you, okay?'

'Okay by me, miss!' shouted a voice and everyone turned to look at Mikey: another big laugh and Kate laughed along, glad that the ice was broken. She launched into the speech she had spent the previous night rehearsing in her room at the pub. A brief outline of the wave technology: how it worked and what the turbines would look like, supported by the illustrations on Declan's easel. She explained how the harbor would need to be enlarged and that cables would need to be run under the main street from the cove. And she emphasized that Ross Oil would improve roads, electricity and water supply, communications and transportation links, all at their own expense. 'Tell them it's a lottery win' – that was Tessa's advice and Kate had taken it to heart. From the smiles and nods she was seeing in the crowd, she felt it was going pretty well. 'So in summary, Ross Oil will bring prosperity to Clover Cove. Jobs, infrastructure and investment. And in return, we will leave the village better than we found it.' She paused and smiled awkwardly. 'Thank you for listening.'

There was a pause, then the church rang with enthusiastic applause.

Declan stepped up next to the table.

'Alright, well I'd like to thank Miss O'Riordan for her presentation. Now I believe she is going to take any questions you might have. If you'd raise your hands, I'll see if I can get to you all.'

'How much money will we get?'

Another laugh. And Kate supposed it was the question they all wanted answering.

'Well, as I said, the benefit to the village will be primarily in the improvement to what's already here. Better roads, more buses, faster broadband. However, I'm guessing you're referring to specific properties that we may have to buy, or pay the owners for access?'

'You're right there.'

A smaller laugh, this one cut by nervous energy. Now they were worried that they might get rich.

'We would negotiate on a case-by-case basis,' said Kate, 'So I couldn't give you a figure here and now. I can say though that Ross Oil will always pay at least twenty per cent over the market value of any property, plus we'd contribute towards relocation, moving costs and so on.'

'Ker-ching!'

'No one's going to buy your hovel, Mikey.'

Declan called for calm and a young man in shirt and tie stood up.

'Danny Brennan, Kilmara Examiner,' he said. 'Miss O'Riordan, you've been talking about this project as a money-making scheme, but isn't it true that it's actually just a PR stunt by Ross Oil to draw attention away from the oil spill scandal in Alaska?'

There were boos and shouts of 'Shut up Danny!'

Kate raised her hands to quiet the crowd.

'I can't comment about the situation in Alaska, but I can say this, Mr. Brennan. Any oil spill brings into sharp focus the problem we all face regarding energy in the 21st century. Fossil fuels are finite and potentially damaging to the environment; Ross Oil has been very open about admitting that. So what Ross Oil wants – what we all want – is a form of energy which is sustainable, clean and has the minimal impact on nature. Now isn't that something to be encouraged?'

There were cheers, but Danny Brennan clearly wasn't placated.

'You haven't answered the question, Miss O'Riordan,' he said over the jeers, 'Isn't this simply a PR stunt to make the fat cats look caring?'

'Let me answer that with a couple of simple facts,' said Kate. 'The biggest electricity generator in Ireland is the coal-fired Moneypoint plant on the Shannon. It also the single biggest contributor to greenhouse emissions in the country. As nuclear power is outlawed in Ireland, renewable energy is the only viable option. Our tidal project carries no danger of meltdown and no toxic waste. Unlike fossil fuels, tidal energy has no ugly rigs, no oil tankers and no pipelines. That is not PR, Mr. Brennan, it is the future of energy.'

A round of jeers and personal insults forced the reporter to sit down.

'What about those of us who don't get our houses bought up? What's in it for us?'

'In previous projects of this nature, Ross Oil has allocated a percentage of profits to create a community fund which can be used any way you choose. In the past we have built schools, a cinema, even a medical clinic; whatever the village needs, it's up to you.'

There was more cheering and a loud shout of 'another pub!' to much laughter. Kate could see Declan looking over at her and she nodded at him.

'Right, I think that gives us all a solid overview of what Ross Oil is proposing,' he said. 'Any final questions?'

Everyone looked around, but no hands were raised.

'Right then, I think...' began Declan, but a hush came over the crowd. Kate looked up and could immediately see why. Connor James was standing in the aisle and all eyes were on him.

'I have a question,' he said in a clear voice.

'Fine,' said Kate, raising her chin defiantly. 'Go ahead.' *Do your worst*, she thought.

'Not for you, Miss O'Riordan,' said Connor. 'For Sir Charles Balcon.'

There was a twitter of whispering and gasps. Kate watched as Charles turned his head to look at Connor.

'I believe Miss O'Riordan came to you yesterday,' said Connor, meeting Charles' gaze, 'And made you a substantial offer of cash to use your land for this project.'

There was a pause.

'That is true, yes.'

'And you turned her down?'

Charles looked at Kate. 'Yes, I did.'

A gasp ran around the church.

'Can you tell us why, Sir Charles?'

Kate felt her stomach drop. She could see Balcon thinking, weighing up his options. Clearly, he didn't want to drop her in it, but his loyalties were to the people in this church.

'I told Miss O'Riordan that I didn't believe the Ross Oil project was in the interest of Clover Cove.'

Uproar. Shouting, cries, insults.

'Why not?' asked Connor, raising his voice.

'That is between myself and Miss O'Riordan.'

'Isn't it true you told her it would destroy the community and ruin the natural beauty of the area?'

The din rose. Kate stood up, waving her hands trying to get order.

'Please, please, let me explain.'

Danny Brennan was on his feet now, waving a Dictaphone.

'Miss O'Riordan, could you comment on the accusation

that had Sir Charles accepted your offer, all the money you're talking about for clinics and schools would have gone straight into his pocket and the residents of Clover Cove would not have seen a penny?'

A roar of noise.

'Isn't that true, Miss O'Riordan?'

'Alright, alright,' shouted Father Declan, jumping up. 'THAT'S ENOUGH!'

Immediately the church fell silent. 'This is the house of THE LORD,' he bellowed, 'And I WILL NOT have you making a MOCKERY of its sanctity.'

A hundred pale faces gaped at him.

'Miss O'Riordan has answered all the questions she is going to tonight. Go back to your homes and sleep on it. Now file out quietly.'

They did as they were told, amid a hum of muttered conversations. Kate saw Declan glare at both Charles and Connor, before turning and leading her to a small room to the side of the altar.

Where she burst into tears.

Chapter 20

Charles Balcon was waiting for Connor as he left the church. Connor had been surrounded by people inside, half wanting to slap him on the back – 'Go on Connor, you tell them son' – and half wanting to ask questions, their faces creased with worry – 'Does this mean there's no money now?'

Connor didn't have any answers, in fact he had a terrible sinking feeling in his stomach that he'd done something wrong and irreversible, so seeing the aristocrat standing there turned his confusion into anger.

'What do you want?' he snapped.

'What was all that in there?' said Charles, blocking Connor's path.

'I asked you a question is all.'

'You humiliated that girl.'

Connor snorted.

'Is that what you're worried about or are you more concerned that *you* looked bad?'

'This is my village, James, and I have no fear that my

standing is strong enough that people will understand that my actions were...'

'Your village?' sneered Connor, his irritation spilling over. '*Your* village? What, you think it's some sort of asset? Something you can buy or sell?'

'No, Connor. But I was born here, just like you. My family has lived in Clover Cove for centuries...'

'And don't we know it? Lording it over us, telling us what to do, taking anything you fancy.'

It was a deliberately loaded comment. The night Ciara had disappeared, she had been seen in Charles Balcon's sportscar. Clearly she hadn't run off with the lord, but he was somehow involved, that was for sure. Their eyes locked, like two dogs circling.

'Don't make this personal,' said Charles. 'You don't know what you're talking about.'

Just then Danny Brennan stepped over, notebook poised and they both turned on him.

'Not now, Danny!' they shouted together.

The reporter flinched, but stood his ground.

'The free press has a right to ask...'

Balcon cut him off with a harsh laugh. 'The free press? Is that what you call it?'

He turned to glare at Connor. 'Enjoy your little victory,' he said. 'But don't think this is the end of it. Not by a country mile.'

He spun on his heel and stalked off towards the square, leaving Connor and Danny alone.

'Could I have a word, Mr. James?' asked Danny timidly.

'*Mr. James*?' laughed Connor, pushing past the reporter and walking down the church path, his feet crunching on the gravel. 'No need to be so formal, Danny. I've known you since you were in nappies.'

Danny had grown up in the Cove, he'd even gone to

school with Ryan, not that that was unusual – all the children in the Cove were bussed out to St. Swithans twelve miles away in Ballymanor. But Ryan had been in Danny's class and they'd been friends although Ryan often referred to him as 'Clever Dick Dan.' Not really a compliment.

'So as a prominent member of the Clover Cove community,' said Danny, flipping over his notebook as he followed Connor down the path, 'Can I take it that you're in opposition to the Ross Oil takeover?'

'The Ross takeover? Danny, it's not the *Dawn of the Dead*. They're not going to enslave us.'

'That's exactly how some people here feel, Mr. James,' said the reporter, pushing his Dictaphone into Connor's face. 'Do you deny you're a supporter of the movement to reject Ross Oil's imperialist land grab?'

'I don't deny anything, in fact I'm not actually telling you anything at all Danny. I'm just me.'

'Come on Connor, you are a pillar of the community in Clover Cove and as such you have a great deal of influence – as we saw in the church.'

Connor stopped and looked at him.

'You really think that?'

The young man frowned. 'Of course.'

'Look Con,' he said, holding up the Dictaphone and making a big show of turning it off, like a gun-fighter laying down his six-shooter. 'Let's talk off the record. You seemed pretty anti the Ross scheme in there. What everyone wants to know is why are you so against it?'

Connor closed his eyes. He knew nothing was ever off the record with Danny Brennan, but he also knew the lad would never leave him alone if he didn't give him something.

'Okay, here's the truth Danny; and I'll thank you to stick to it without embellishment, okay? I actually wasn't 'anti' when I came to the meeting, I genuinely came with an open mind. I'm not against the oil people per se, but I spoke up because I was concerned that only one side of the argument was being put forward: the Ross Oil side.'

'And you really think they're going to steal the soul of the village, eh?'

'Not my words, Danny. But I do think they'll change the way the Cove looks, the way we go about our lives and it'll change the make-up of the Cove.'

'And that's a bad thing?'

'Isn't it?'

'I'm just the reporter, Con. I'm here to report. But I can tell you that there are plenty of people who'd welcome the Ross Oil money. Clover Cove isn't exactly flush, is it?'

'True enough. But that doesn't mean we have to do a deal with the devil.'

He saw Danny's face light up. '*Off* the record, remember Danny? Now don't go writing I said that Ross Oil is the devil...' he began, but Danny wasn't looking at him. Connor turned and saw Declan standing there, giving the reporter one of his hard stares. But Danny clearly hadn't noticed, his attention was elsewhere.

'Yeah, thanks Connor, speak to you later...' he said vaguely.

'Well how d'ya like that?' said Connor, watching the lad drift away, his gaze fixed on a girl with blonde hair tied back in a red scarf. Ah, Tessa the artist. Connor smiled to himself. She was certainly a pretty girl and at least it showed the boy's mind wasn't entirely focused on grabbing a scoop.

'A word, Con,' said Declan, nodding his head back towards the church.

'Ah Dec, can you keep the sermon for Sunday?' sighed

Connor. 'I've had enough of having my ear being bent for one night.'

'I think you'll want to listen to this,' he said, beckoning.

Reluctantly, Connor followed the priest through into the vestry, a room at the side of the altar he'd once heard Declan refer to as the 'backstage area.'

Waiting there for him was Kate O'Riordan.

Connor groaned and began to back out, but Declan closed the door, the key clicking in the lock.

'Ah come on,' said Connor, 'What is this, an ambush?'

'You're a fine one to talk about ambushes,' said Kate, folding her arms.

'What do you mean?'

'Don't play innocent with me, Connor. You destroyed my meeting in there. I had everyone on my side and you ruined everything!'

Connor laughed.

'I ruined it? Whatever happened in there was your own doing, Kate O'Riordan.'

'Don't try and deny you went to that meeting with the sole intention of derailing my chances of making this project work.'

'No!' he barked, then closed his eyes and took a deep breath. 'Look, I will admit I don't think Ross Oil is good for Clover Cove. But I honestly went in there to hear what you had to say and let the people make up their own minds.'

'So why stand up and make that crack about Sir Charles?'

'Because you lied, Kate!'

'Lied?'

'You led the villagers to believe that all those things – the kiddies playground, the hospital – were part of the deal. Be honest, would anything have been built if your money had gone to Charles Balcon?'

Kate's face went red and she looked as if she was about to explode.

'YES!' she shouted, 'Of course they would! The school, the clinic, it would still have happened whoever we gave our money to.'

Connor looked at her in confusion.

'Oh, do some research, Connor,' said Kate, 'This isn't the first time Ross Oil has had to run a pipeline or build a plant in a new place. We're not idiots, we know the best way to make it work is to keep people happy by sharing the wealth.'

Connor gaped at her.

'So why didn't you say so?'

'Because you didn't give me a chance!' she shouted. 'And now it's too late. If I go back and say, 'yes, of course you can have your cinema or your library,' everyone will think Ross Oil are these greedy manipulative bullies trying to buy their way into the village. So well done Connor, you've won.'

'I just wanted to see the best done for the village.'

'The best for the village or the best for you?'

'This is nothing to do with me!'

'But it is, Connor. People here respect you and your opinion, they were looking to you to guide them. Well congratulations, you certainly did that.'

Connor had that sinking feeling again, the nagging suspicion that he'd messed up. Still, he didn't appreciate how she was laying it on so thick.

'Don't be a sore loser,' he said.

Kate put her hands on her hips.

'You know what drives me mad about you, Connor? You maintain his pose of caring about the community, but what you actually care about is you and your position in it.'

'You're wrong.'

'Am I? Then why are you so frightened to have anything change here?

He began to answer, but realized he couldn't.

'Look Kate... I'm just trying my best. Can't you give me a break here?'

She shook her head wearily.

'It doesn't matter Connor. I can see you're protective of the Cove – you should be, it's a lovely corner of the world. But can't you see this was a chance to make it better? To give it a future?'

'What kind of future? One that suits Ross Oil?'

'Of course it suits Ross Oil!' she cried, throwing her hands in the air. 'We're not a charity, Connor! We wanted to come here to make money, sure. And yes, Danny Brennan's right, we do like good publicity. What's so wrong about any of that?'

He looked away.

'Maybe I value other things.'

'Okay, great. But are your principles about community going to hold this place together, Connor? It's a noble cause, but don't you think Clover Cove needs a clinic and a school?'

'Sure, but...'

'And how are you going to get them without money? And what happens when the bar has to close?'

He looked at her sharply. 'How do you...?'

Kate laughed bitterly, shaking her head.

'Don't get so worked up. I haven't been hacking into your bank accounts. Anyone can see that you're struggling.'

He bristled. What business was that of hers?

'We're going through a tough time, that's all.'

'I heard the delivery man yesterday. He said you're way behind on your payments.'

Connor looked down at the floor, ashamed, but Kate stepped over and gently touched his arm.

'You're a kind man Connor, underneath it all,' she said. 'You let people run a tab, give them free meals at the bar. And I heard how you helped Mrs. Brennan with her flowers yesterday. You didn't need to do that.'

Connor's shame turned to embarrassment.

'You do what you can.'

'Exactly, Connor. And it's great that the pub is the centre of the community. But if there's no work, no industry, no tourism, then your customers – your community – have no money and you end up supporting them instead of the other way around. And what happens when your money runs out?'

'We'll manage. We always have. My Da...'

Kate lifted a hand and pointed at him. 'And there it is.'

'There's what?

'There's the root of the problem. You're not your father, Connor. And you don't have to do things the same way.'

'Don't you speak about him! He was a great man!'

Her voice, her face softened.

'I'm sure he was. But we live in different times. If he was here, maybe he'd have done things differently too.'

'You're saying my Da would have given in to Ross Oil?'

Kate threw her head back and shouted in frustration.

'NO Connor! I don't know, I never met the man. I'm saying you have to live your own life and make your own decisions. And you'll have to live with this one when I've gone.'

His eyes opened wide.

'You're leaving?'

She looked at him in disbelief.

'Of course I'm leaving! I've failed, Connor. I've failed to persuade his Lordship, failed to persuade the de facto mayor, failed to get the support of the Cove. And all in the space of a few days.' Kate gave a weak laugh. 'Personal record. It usually takes me at least a few weeks to screw things up this badly.'

'Kate, I...'

She waved a hand and turned away. 'Don't sweat it, Connor James. You won. Great.' She opened the door leading into the church, then turned back. 'Oh, and I'll be checking out in the morning. Just so you know.'

Connor watched her go, wondering why it felt like someone had dropped a rock onto his chest.

Chapter 21

It seemed fitting really. The rain was humming down on the square, the puddles pocked and shimmering, just like her first day in Clover Cove.

And my last, Kate thought as she stepped out of the side door, her borrowed Wellingtons slap-slapping on the path. Once again she was up with the sunrise, having been unable to sleep, going over and over the church meeting in her head. Where had she gone wrong? What could she have done differently? Everything. And what was so galling was that she had been so *close*. Before that self-interested oaf Connor James had stepped in, Kate could feel it going her way. The village had been on her side.

She sighed and flipped up the hood on the cast-off coat. It didn't really matter now, did it? The whole thing was over. After her confrontation with Connor in the vestry, she had gone straight back to her room and, suddenly blessed with a full signal – of course: there's always a great connection when you need to send bad news – had contacted the office to fill them in; 'no dice in Clover Cove, better start looking for another site.' *And I'd better start looking for another job.*

She supposed it had always been a risk and, frankly, she had come to Ireland as much to get away from Manhattan – and David – as take on the project, but even so, Kate couldn't help but feel she had let herself down. Herself, and the people of Clover Cove. Whatever Connor James and his friends in the bar thought, the Ross Oil deal would have been good for the village. The Cove was beautiful and unique, but it desperately needed dragging into the 21st century. You couldn't live in the past forever.

Still, right now Clover Cove was pretty. She walked slowly down the lane towards the harbor, looking at the still dark windows of the shops and houses, thinking of all people she had met in the short few days she'd spent in Clover Cove. Molly, Raff, Tessa. Father Dec. The funny thing was, Kate had felt at home here. Not welcomed exactly, but there was something about the place. Something magical.

Kate stopped at the harbor. The rain was easing off and the view was lovely; perhaps more so because of the wind still drawing swirls and ripples on the surface of the water.

She glanced at the buildings along the front. Molly's café was still shuttered and no light came from Tessa's studio. Kate didn't like goodbyes, but she didn't feel right about leaving without seeing her new friends. She looked at her watch. Perhaps there would be time later. Or perhaps it was better just to go and leave this all behind her.

She walked onto the beach, hands deep in her pockets, wading the ankle-deep gullies between the wind-blown ridges in the sand. Kate was glad of her boots – without them, she'd be up to her knees. That made her think of Connor James and their walk along the clifftops the first day. He'd been so intense, so in tune with his surroundings. 'If only I had known what he was really like…' she whispered to herself. Maybe she'd been projecting some ideal onto him, some traits she wanted to see that weren't there. God, he was maddening!

A movement caught her attention and Kate lifted her hood to get a better look: yes, someone was on the far side of the beach. They were crouching down, like a child playing in a rock pool. Curious, Kate began to amble that way. Though the sun was still behind cloud, it had brightened, making Kate shield her eyes to see.

'Tessa? Is that you?'

The blonde girl looked up and beamed.

'Kate! How lovely. What are you doing up so early?'

She shrugged. 'Couldn't sleep.'

Tessa gave her a sympathetic look. 'Yes, I imagine. Did you speak to…?'

'Connor? Yes, I gave him a piece of my mind.'

Tessa smiled.

'No, I meant did you tell your office?'

'Ah. Yes, I left a message with my boss. Might as well have given him my resignation.'

'Oh, it's not all that bad is it? Surely this sort of thing happens all the time, doesn't it?'

'Not to me. And anyway, I kind of asked for the assignment, said I'd make it happen. Doesn't look good either way.'

Tessa seemed to make the logical conclusion.

'You're not leaving already?'

Kate nodded. 'Came down to have one last walk – and to say goodbye. I'm sure glad I bumped into you.' She frowned. 'Actually, why *are* you down here so early?'

Tessa lifted a kit-bag she was holding. 'Art materials,' she said, reaching inside. 'Just the basics: shells… some fishing net.... Driftwood... that's a nice shape, don't you think?'

'Wow, beats going into the office.'

'You'd think that, wouldn't you? But my butt is frozen and I've got green slime on my jeans, so it's not for everyone.'

Kate looked up towards the cliffs. 'Well, I for one envy you all this. I will miss the Cove.'

'The Cove or the people?'

'Both. It's had its moments. This beach, meeting you, Molly, Raff, Father Dec.'

Tessa lifted an eyebrow.

'And Connor?'

Kate looked at her. '*Definitely* not.'

'Really? Because, well...'

'Well what?'

Tessa looked at her, jaw set.

'Okay, okay. None of my business. So when are you leaving?'

'Soon as I've had a walk up around the headland; one last look. Nothing to keep me here now.'

'If you say so. Well, how about a farewell skinny decaf cappuccino at Molly's on your way back?'

'It's a date.'

She walked off down the sand and turned to see the footprints she was leaving behind her, but the sand was so wet they were melting back into the beach, leaving only vague indentations filling with water. Just like Kate had never been there. *Perhaps that's for the best,* she thought. *In fact, maybe, just maybe, Connor James was right after all.* At this time of day, the Cove was so beautiful, so pristine and untouched by time or man, it seemed obscene to even consider changing it. Kate knew that wasn't the whole story of course and she knew – no doubt even Connor James suspected the same thing – that something had to change in Clover Cove if the village was to survive. But as it was now out of her hands, Kate felt a sneaking sense of relief. On vacation the previous year, Kate had visited the Grand Canyon, which, if you could ignore the vast coach parties, was obviously magnificent. But she had hated the new glass walkway that had been built over the mile-long drop. It was architecturally tasteful and unquestionably impressive as a feat of engineering but it was... just wrong. It had taken most of the drive back to Phoenix before Kate had been able to put her finger on what had really bothered her about it. It wasn't the queues or the ice cream stalls, it wasn't even the arrogance of thinking that one of the natural wonders of the world could be improved by a sideshow costing twenty-eight bucks. No, it was the fact that it was so out of place. The steel and glass and tile, none of it belonged there. It was like tying a bow on a lily or adding fairy lights to a Michelangelo.

And that was how she felt about Clover Cove. The deep irony was that this was Kate's job; she came into untouched places and changed them. She had worked on Ross Oil projects all around the world. There was a dam in Kenya, a pipeline in Norway, even an award-winning refinery perched on the Oregon coast, which even Kate could admit was an eyesore. And none of them had bothered her before.

So why care more about Clover Cove? Perhaps it was because she felt so at home here. Perhaps there *was* something in her grandfather's talk about being connected to the emerald isle after all. Kate had assumed it was nostalgia on gramps' part; it's easy to fool yourself into looking at your youth through rose-tinted spectacles. But there *was* something about this place. Maybe its spirit was part of her. Or maybe it was just pretty. It was certainly that.

She had come to the end of beach now, where the headland jutted out into the sea, but she wasn't ready to go back yet. Who knew when – or if – she'd be back here? Kate wanted to fix it all in her mind's eye, a vivid memory she could take away with her. She climbed over some rocks and found herself on a narrow strip of sand being lapped by the wind-scuffed waves. Glancing up at the clifftops, Kate could see where she was; on the other side of the headland she'd be able to see Sleagh Castle and the little bay Connor had taken her to on that first morning. Battleship Bay? No, *Ironship* Bay. She wanted to see the puffins one more time, so she pushed on, jumping over rock pools and clambering across a flat black rock pocked with barnacles.

'There,' she grinned as she jumped down onto the sand. The other side of the headland was just as pretty, if not more so. More dramatic, more wild. The wind was slanting in from the south-west and caught her hair, whipping it into her face, but that just added to the drama. The beach wasn't as wide here, so Kate had to scramble over boulders and patches of pebbles strewn with seaweed and the sort of sea-washed debris Tessa gathered for her sculptures. As she moved, Kate kept her eyes trained on the cliffs above her, looking for the birds. There were plenty to see; she recognized the guillemots from their wing shape as they hovered, then plunged into the water. It was thrilling to see nature in the raw, completely unconcerned by her presence, just going about their day-to-day business of nest-building, hunting and feeding, all the while keeping up a raucous conversation of squawks and cries. It was like being in a foreign marketplace, listening to the hawkers as they haggled with customers, lost in the hubbub and chaos. She loved it.

The wind whipped her coat and she slipped, one foot treading into a pool with a sploosh. Kate looked down at the lapping waves that hadn't been there a few minutes ago; then turned and saw with mounting concern that while she had been entranced by the spectacle on the cliffs, the tide had turned. It was coming in. Fast.

'Oh no,' she whispered, quickly climbing up out of the water then awkwardly she made her way back towards the jutting headland, having to take a higher route each time: the patches of sand she'd skipped across were gone now, swallowed by the incoming sea. She wasn't even halfway back to the beach when Kate had to admit to herself that she wasn't going to be able to get back that way, not without swimming. What had been yellow sand lapped by gentle waves was now full sea crashing against the foot of the cliffs, a tumble of jagged rocks far too steep to climb. She was trapped.

'Okay, don't panic,' she whispered to herself. 'It's not a storm, it's just high tide. It happens every day, right? I just need to go the other way.' But Kate immediately saw that it would be worse going back into the narrow bay. The sea cave that had been so thrilling that morning with Connor had sides of mossy green rock rising to a sharp overhang: even if she had been an experienced mountain climber, Kate doubted she'd be able to scale that slick wet rock. And soon that cave would be filled with booming waves.

Her heart began to pound as she craned her neck looking for a route up the cliff. *Oh no.* There was no path, no helpful bushes to hold onto, just slippery, sharp slabs of rock backed by vertical cliffs. It was impossible. She looked over her shoulder, back at where the beach had been; the waves were rushing into the little cove higher and higher and the rock Kate had been standing on was already half underwater.

Kate could hear her heart in her ears now, her breath was ragged. This was serious. Deadly serious. She was cold and wet and even if she could stay out of the rising water, she knew that people actually died from hypothermia. In Manhattan, she'd just hail a cab or shelter in a diner, but this wasn't Manhattan, was it?

'Keep it together,' she whispered to herself. Hysteria wasn't going to help. There was simply no choice: she had to try and climb.

The first few rocks were fine, it was just a matter of picking the right route up, but the closer Kate got to the cliff-face, the less she could see. She had to lean back to see anything and twice almost overbalanced backwards: only by pin-wheeling her arms and clutching at the loose rock did she steady herself. To make matters worse, the wind was rising, bringing spray from below to soak Kate's already-wet clothes and making her fingers stiff and numb.

'Help!' she shouted, feeling the futility of it, but she had to do something. 'Heeellllpp!' She stopped, waiting for a reply, but all she heard was the splash of water on rocks, the ghostly whistle of the wind and the mocking cries of the birds. Kate reached up, catching hold of a rock, which immediately crumbled, making her jerk back, her toes slipping from the narrow ledge on which she had been standing. She slid down, knees and palms tearing, desperately jamming her fingernails into the rock. It worked: or at least it held her long enough to get a foothold and prevent a head-over-heels pitch into the sea. Panting, she hugged the cliff face, her arms and legs shaking, knowing that she was stuck.

But being stuck wasn't an option. She was shivering now, both from cold and genuine fear. She had to climb. *Had* to. She reached up, grasping the rock, ignoring the pain as the sharp stones bit into her hands. Scrabbling with her toes, she found purchase and forced herself upwards, then did it again. One hold at a time. Take it slowly. *Yes, you can do this.* Another step, and another. She dared to look up.

The cliff was closer, still far, but closer. Another handhold, feel with your toes. And up. For a moment, Kate dared to hope that she might actually make it. Then something exploded in front of her. She just had time to register the feathers and beak. And then she was falling.

Chapter 22

Raff's boat was tiny, pinkie-nail size and half-hidden by the curtain of rain shimmering over the water. Standing on the cliff path, Connor looked beyond the fishing trawler at the bank of dark clouds fast closing in on the cove.

'Run, Raff,' he said to himself. 'Get back to the harbor before it hits.'

He'll be grand, Connor thought. Raff had spent his whole life on this stretch of coastline, he knew every sand-bank and eddy. Raff could tell the weather by smell alone and had won more than a few pints from unsuspecting tourists to prove it. Raff would have seen the storm coming and timed his journey home to the minute.

But things happened at sea, even to the best sailors; everyone in Clover Cove knew that, Connor more than most. Mother Nature had a way of slapping you when you were looking the other way. Right on cue, a gust of wind swept up over the cliffs and Connor flipped up his collar. A bit of cold wasn't going to turn him back, not yet anyway.

He strode on, hands deep in his pockets. A hike along the coast path often helped him calm his restless mind and today it was buzzing with questions. *What could I have done differently? Did I mess the whole thing up?* And right at the forefront: *is Kate really leaving?* Kate O'Riordan. The very thought of her made Connor's chest hurt. She drove him mad with her certainty about everything. She didn't seem to doubt – even for one moment – that she was wrong. She was so stubborn and unbending in her belief that Ross Oil was good for Clover Cove. And yet the thought of her leaving forever made Connor feel like someone had punched him in the stomach. Why? He'd only known the girl a matter of days and he'd spent most of that time butting heads. It didn't make any sense.

But love doesn't make sense, does it Con? Said a voice in his head, a voice he recognized. It was Ciara, the girl who had broken his heart. And that was what she had said to him on their last night together: 'love doesn't make any sense.' Her justification for walking out of his life. Whatever he'd said, however much he'd begged, she gave him that. Just because you love someone to hell's gate, it doesn't mean they're going to love you back. Not as much, anyway. Not enough.

Especially when they love someone else.

Connor was standing on the edge of the cliff now, the wind pushing against him. He could hear the boom of the waves charging into the sea cave and the cries of the gulls. *Ah, Ciara, why'd you have to...*

Connor stopped, frowning. That wasn't a gull.

He turned his head, trying to duck the wind, trying to pick out that cry he'd heard. For a moment, Connor thought he'd been imagining it, just another voice in his head. But there it was again: a human voice.

Coming from below.

'Hello?' He cried, cupping his hands around his mouth. 'Who's there?'

He listened: nothing but the wind. Concerned now, Connor lay down on the cliff's edge, searching the bay below. Not that there was much of it left: the tide was rushing in, the white-tipped waves charging one after the other like a stampede. Just wet, jagged rocks and – there! A dark shape at the base of the cliff just below him.

'Hold tight!' he shouted. 'I'm coming down.'

He quickly stripped off his jacket and stuffed it in a hollow where the wind couldn't grab it, then turned and backed over the edge of the cliff. As a young lad, Connor had led a gang of kids all over these cliffs, pretending to be commandos or smugglers. It had been a while for sure, but he remembered the best routes to avoid overhangs and crumbling scree. Sure-footed, he quickly clambered down until he was standing on a ledge of rock. It was solid enough, but the crashing waves and the incoming storm had made everything damp and slippery. Connor could now see the figure below, clinging desperately to a mossy boulder that would soon be engulfed by the incoming waves.

'Hey down there!' he called. 'Can you move?'

There was a tight shake of the head. Connor could feel the tension even from twenty feet above; they were locked up by fear and exhaustion.

'No worries, I'll be down in a tick,' he called, but he took it slowly now. The rock was sheer, having been pounded smooth by the relentless sea, and hand-holds were few. Finally, he was within an arm's length.

'Here, you'll have to reach up and take my hand,' he shouted. The roaring sea was all but drowning his words now, but he saw the figure unfold, a white hand stretching towards him. Connor twisted to grasp it, but the movement made his boot slip, sending a shower of earth down over the head of the stranded man.

Only it wasn't a man. A shrill string of insults was

directed his way, suggesting he might like to watch where he was stepping.

'Sorry,' he began, then did a double take as he recognized that voice.

'*Kate*?'

'Of course it's me,' she yelled. 'Now pull me up before we both drown!'

Connor was about to laugh, when a wave sliced across the cliff-face, drenching them both. He looked up: the sky was fully dark now. The storm would hit them within minutes and if they weren't off the rocks, they would both be in real danger.

'Quickly,' he said, lowering his hand again. Without hesitation, Kate grasped his wrist and he hauled her up, just as another wave broke below. Connor pulled her face to face with him, his arm circling her waist.

'Hello there,' he said. 'Get lost?'

'Looking for puffins,' she said.

Kate was shivering, her body cold against his. She was being brave, but she must have been terrified.

'Connor?' she said, her teeth chattering.

'Yes?'

'Can we go?'

He smiled at that. 'Sure, but...'

'But what?' Her eyes were wide with fear.

'This part could be tricky,' said Connor, 'I need two hands for this next bit, so you're going to have to trust me, okay? Put your arms around my neck so I can climb.'

She did as she was told, wrapping her legs around his hips, her cold cheek against his exposed neck. He heard her bite back a squeal as he began to climb, but she held on. *Good girl,* he thought, because he needed every ounce of strength and concentration as he pushed upwards, step by step. Her weight was making holds slip and give way, but it was the effect on his balance that was the biggest threat: their centre of gravity pulling them both away from the rock. His legs burnt and shook, his fingers were numb as he dug into the loose earth nearer the cliff edge. But then, finally, there it was. The top.

'Allez oop!' he grunted and scrambled over the grassy edge and they collapsed full-length on the grass. Kate still clung to him, her whole body shaking.

'Thank you,' she whispered, her voice gravelly. Then she began to sob. 'I thought...'

'Hey now,' said Connor, pushing wet hair from her face. 'Don't take on so. We made it. You're okay.'

'But I... if you hadn't been there...' she gulped.

'Ah, but I was there, wasn't I? I came to watch the puffins too – always do when I...'

He frowned and looked away, annoyed with himself. He'd said too much. He sat up, scrabbling across to where he'd left his jacket, wrapping it around Kate's shoulders. For a moment, they sat that way, Connor rubbing warmth back into her back and arms. When she stopped shaking, Kate turned towards him.

'Connor?' she asked softly. 'Tell me. Why did you come here?'

Connor closed his eyes, shook his head.

'I always come up here when I need to think,' he said reluctantly. 'I sometimes come here to... no, it's stupid.'

'Tell me.'

Her face was pale, but open. Sincere. Ah, what did it matter? The girl would be gone tomorrow.

'You'll think I'm crazy,' he sighed. 'But when I have something on my mind, I come to talk to my Da.' He glanced at her to gauge her reaction. 'Silly isn't it? It's like he's out there in the sea still, listening.'

He blew out his cheeks and smiled. 'He never talks back, mind.'

Kate didn't smile.

'He... he was killed at sea?'

Connor nodded.

'Back when the Cove still lived by fishing, the village had a lifeboat. If anyone was in trouble out at sea, they'd send up a flare and the volunteers would drop whatever they were doing to man the lifeboat. That day, there was a gale blowing past the 'head and two boats were taking on water, threatening to go down. As it happened, they both made it back. My Da...' He shook his head. Kate reached out and touched his hand. He flinched slightly, then relaxed.

'I think it's nice,' she said pushing herself up next to him, her body warm now. 'Nice that you come out here to talk to him. I feel the same way about my granddad.'

'Oh, I'm sorry. When did he pass?'

'Oh, he's not dead. He just moved to Florida.'

Connor nodded, holding her gaze, then he couldn't help himself: he burst out laughing. Kate joined in and Connor felt the tension ease a little. She moulded herself to him and he pulled her as close as he dared, willing the moment to last forever. But it couldn't; it was raining now and the wind was snatching at their hair. They needed to get down to the village before the full force of the storm hit.

'Come on,' said Connor reluctantly, pushing to his feet and helping Kate up. But he didn't let go of her hand.

'Listen Kate,' he said, 'I want to apologize.'

She raised her eyebrows. 'You?'

'Don't laugh,' he said, 'I just... maybe I could have gone about this in a different way. You're right that Clover Cove needs something to happen, to change for the better. The people here, they're my family and I don't want to stand in their way. And...'

He paused, fearing the anguish was showing on his face. *Say it, man,* he thought fiercely. *Say it.*

'And I don't want you to go.'

She looked at him in surprise.

'You don't?'

'No Kate,' he said softly, reaching up to touch her cheek, 'I don't.'

'But what about...?'

Connor felt it all happen in slow motion. His hand slipping around her neck, gently pulling her closer, his head tilting, Kate's eyes closing, anticipating the warm brush of his lips. Then he stopped.

Kate opened one eye.

'Connor?' she asked.

Connor frowned, holding up a finger. 'Do you hear that?'

'Hear what?' said Kate, her confusion plain.

Connor turned south, shielding his eyes.

'There,' he said. The noise was clear now: a grinding 'whup-whup-whup', getting closer. A helicopter. Had someone seen Kate on the rocks and called the Coast Guard? But as the helicopter came into view, it wasn't the distinctive red and white of the search and rescue choppers. It was blue, with strange white markings on the side.

'It's one of ours,' said Kate.

'Yours?' called Connor, having to raise his voice over the growing rattle of the helicopter blades.

'Look at the logo on the side,' cried Kate, pointing up at the aircraft that was now circling overhead. 'It's a Ross Oil chopper!'

The grass on the clifftop was being whipped and flattened as the helicopter circled one more time and slid towards them.

'It's landing!' Kate shouted.

Connor took her hand and pulled her further away from the edge; didn't want her being swept over after all. They watched as the helicopter's wheels gently touched down and the door opened. A man in a suit stepped out, holding a briefcase, his tie whipping crazily back and forth. He bent and ran towards them, a grin on his face.

'Pretty dramatic entrance, huh?' he shouted, pulling Kate into an awkward embrace. Over the man's shoulder, Kate's eyes met Connor's.

'Connor, I...' she began, but the stone in his stomach told him everything he needed to know. The helicopter man turned, as if noticing Connor for the first time.

'David Schwartz,' he said, thrusting his hand forward. 'Ross Oil.'

Connor couldn't think of anything to say.

'David, what are you doing here?' said Kate.

The man threw up his hands in a gesture of modesty.

'What else?' he smiled, 'I'm here to save the day.'

Chapter 23

Kate closed the door of her room and watched as David crossed to the window, peering out at the storm.

'David, what the hell are you doing here? Seriously.'

He turned, a self-satisfied smiled on his face.

'Leo sent me to close the deal,' he said, as if it was obvious. But didn't make any sense, not to Kate anyway. She tried to rewind the timeline in her mind.

'When did he send you? And more importantly: why?'

David gave an exaggerated shrug.

'Alright, so I asked to come,' he said, 'What can I say? I miss you, Kate.'

Kate shook her head: it still didn't add up.

'But Clover Cove is a dead duck. We had a meeting in the church last night. I put the Ross proposal to the village and I was shouted down. I left a message at head office, didn't you get it?'

'Sure, but it ain't over until the Big D says it's over,' he said. Kate knew that smug look. She narrowed her eyes.

'What's happened, David?'

David flipped out a hand like a magician revealing a card.

'I cut a deal. It's what I do.'

'Who with? Who cut a deal?'

'Your friend Sir Charles.'

Kate's eyes opened wide.

'You've seen him already?'

David nodded, looked down at his perfectly manicured nails. 'This morning, that's where I was coming from in the chopper, breakfast meeting. Did you even know they had a Michelin-starred restaurant in this godforsaken backwater?'

'But how? He was at the meeting last night and Sir Charles was still against the project.'

David grinned. 'You reckoned without Mrs. Schwartz's boy,' said David, cocking a thumb against his chest. 'Although I have to admit your little meeting did a lot of the groundwork. Seems someone rattled Sir Chuck's cage last night – he was still steaming this morning.'

He walked over to the dresser and picked up a ceramic cow, looking at it as if it were a curio dug out of a pyramid.

'So when you dropped that message about your meeting with Sir Charles, all I heard was the word "money." If some Brit wants to play hardball, he's come to the right place.'

'But he wanted a fortune.'

'Sure, but Leo gave me this.'

David dropped the cow and held up his hand, finger and thumb pinched as if he were holding something.

'What's that David?' she said impatiently.

'A blank check, baby. So I jumped on the company jet, grabbed the chopper and waved the money at Chuck.' He gave a sly smile and wagged a finger at her. 'I think Sir Charles is a little sweet on you, honey. And who can blame him?'

Kate waved an impatient hand.

'He wasn't that sweet a few days ago, in fact he seemed pretty adamant he didn't want us here.'

David chuckled.

'I made him an offer he couldn't refuse.'

'You threatened him?'

He shook his head.

'Zeroes, baby. All it took was the right amount of zeroes.'

Irritating though David was, Kate was still invested in the development and couldn't help feeling excited.

'So what's the deal?' she said. 'Are we using the cliffs or going under the headland? And did you talk about siting a dock? We'll still need somewhere for the maintenance ships...'

David put up a hand.

'Details, Katie. That's your department. The headline is we got the deal.'

'We? I'm still on the project?'

'Of course. This is a win-win for both of us.'

Kate shook her head.

'Oh no. There is no "us," David. You made that very clear back in New York.'

David stepped towards her, touching her arm. Kate made an effort not to recoil.

'I'm big enough to admit I was wrong,' he said, tilting his head in a display of sincerity. 'I was stupid, impetuous.'

'Impetuous?' she laughed, 'Did you look that up?'

'Hey, cut me some slack Katie, I made a big, big mistake, but we're good together, you know that. And Leo likes you, he sees you as the daughter he never had.'

Ah, thought Kate. Now we're getting to the truth. Typical David: he'd tried to maneuver Kate off the project, but when he realized the CEO was still behind her, he'd changed tack.

'So this isn't a relationship, it's a career move for you.'

Kate was surprised when David simply shrugged.

'Why fight it, Kate? We can be the power couple of Ross Oil. They're always saying how there aren't enough women on the board. With me at your side, you can go all the way.'

She began to object, but he pressed a finger to her lips.

'Don't say anything. Why don't you think about it, huh? I think you'll see it makes sense for both of us.'

He flashed her what he clearly believed was a winning smile and opened the door with a flourish.

'I'll see you down in the bar, huh?'

When he was gone. Kate let out a long breath, then sank down onto the bed. He was aggravating and full of himself, but she had to admit there was something appealing about David's cynical game-playing. Sure, it was no girl's idea of romance, but where had romance ever got her? And what else was she going to do? Resign? She couldn't leave David in charge – he'd dynamite the cliffs and cover the beach in concrete. At least this way she got to stay in the village and maybe even make amends by funneling some of the budget towards projects that might benefit the residents. *And what about Connor?* said the voice in her head.

On the walk down from the cliffs to the village, he'd been sullen and silent, not that she could exactly blame him. In that moment just before the helicopter had appeared in the distance, Kate had been sure he was about to kiss her. He *had*, hadn't he? And he'd told her he wanted her to stay. But did it mean anything? Hadn't it just been the drama of the moment? People did things like that when they'd been in crisis situations, she'd read about it in *Time*.

Kate sighed. She was caught between the devil and the deep blue sea, almost literally. She could only stay in Clover Cove if she agreed to David's bargain and even if Connor had meant that kiss, she'd still have to leave. She'd have no job and even if she resigned, with the Ross Oil project going ahead, her presence in the village would be impossible.

She walked into the bathroom and gasped at the reflection looking back at her. No wonder Connor didn't kiss her. Her hair was tangled and plastered down on one side, there were bright red spots in the middle of her cheeks – matching her nose – and there was mud and dried blood where she'd hit herself on the ledge. *At least there's no bird poop,* she thought, grabbing the soap and doing her best to make herself at least presentable. Finally, Kate left the room and took the creaky stairs down to the pub, still no wiser about what to do next.

'Ah, so it is yourself Miss Kate,' said Raff warmly as she pushed through the door. 'Come and sit next to me, let me buy you a drink.'

Kate glanced around the bar; it was busy and the air was filled with excitement. No great surprise. It wasn't every day a helicopter landed on the cliffs. She waved to Tessa and Molly sitting by the fire; no need for that farewell coffee anymore, she supposed. Connor was hunched at the end of the bar, talking into the telephone and David was over the other side of the room talking to Danny Brennan, no doubt giving him the good news about benevolent Ross Oil and how it was going to bring prosperity to the area. *Stop,* she scolded herself. Hadn't she been spinning the exact same line at the meeting last night?

'Sure, a drink would be nice,' said Kate, sitting on the stool next to Raff. 'But none of your "black stuff" this time. Maybe just tea: I could do with warming up.'

'Tea? Meh! We need whiskey!' he said, clapping his hands. 'We can't toast your big news with a cup of tea.'

She looked up to see if Connor was listening, but he

was still talking intently on the telephone, his hand covering the mouthpiece.

'Well, I guess it *is* good news that the tidal project is going ahead after all,' said Kate carefully. 'I know some people weren't entirely convinced by it, but I hope we'll prove to you all...'

'Not that news,' said Raff in a stage whisper, rolling his eyes towards David. 'The *big* news.'

'What big news?'

Raff gave her a conspiratorial wink.

'Oh, I know you've got to keep it under wraps until you've spoken to your folks, but you're among friends here, Miss Kate.' He nudged her and pointed down, Under the bar, Raff spread his left hand, then tapped the third finger.

Kate's eyes opened wide in astonishment and Raff grinned. 'Yer man told us,' he said, nodding towards David.

'David?' hissed Kate, 'He told you we were getting... *married*?'

Raff patted her knee. 'Your secret's safe with us, darlin'.'

'With *us*?' said Kate. 'Who else has David told?'

'Oh, he told the whole bar.'

She looked up at Connor in alarm, just in time to see him hang up the phone and disappear through the door to the hotel.

'Sorry Raff, we'll have that drink later,' said Kate, jumping up. She pushed through into the back just as Connor was stepping out the back door.

'Connor! Wait!'

She saw him hesitate for a moment, then turn away, slamming the door behind him. Kate made to follow, fumbling with the latch, then realized she had nothing on her feet; she had left her muddy wellingtons boots by the door. Stifling a curse, she ran across and pulled on the boots, but by the time she was outside, Connor had gone. Shoulders hunched against the rain, she ran to the back of the pub and spotted a gap in a hedge. Beyond it was a narrow pathway running behind the cottages and she sprinted over. One way went towards the sea, the other toward the church, just peeking out above the trees. On a hunch, Kate chose the church, splashing through puddles, not even sure what she would say even if she caught up with him. But right then, it just felt like the only thing that mattered in the world.

'Connor, please! Stop!' Kate had reached a rusty gate leading to the little churchyard and Connor was approaching the arched door of the vestry. She saw him stop, his shoulders rounded, head down. Finally, he turned, pushing his hands deep into the pockets of his coat, a picture of surly reluctance. But Kate knew she needed to set the record straight. She clambered over the stile, landing with as much dignity as over-sized wellington boots would allow and quickly ran over. The rain was lashing down now, soaking her again.

'Listen, I don't know what David has been telling you, but I'm sure he's got his wires crossed somewhere.'

Connor pulled a face. 'Not my business, is it?'

'I just wanted to say that we're not – that is, David and I...'

He held up a hand.

'Kate, you don't have to say anything to me.'

'I know, but I want to. I want you to know.'

He shook his head emphatically, droplets of water falling to the ground.

'I don't have any hold over you. You're free to go and do whatever you want, aren't you?'

She blinked at him.

'Why are you being like this? Up there on the cliffs, I thought something happened. It *did* Connor, didn't it?'

'But that was before yer man flew down from the clouds, wasn't it? Seems in all the excitement you'd forgotten about him.'

'Forgotten? We're not – David isn't my boyfriend, Connor!'

'No, he's your fiance, isn't he?'

She opened her mouth to object, but Connor plowed on. 'Look Kate, it's fine. You'd had a fright on the rocks, you were feeling vulnerable, I shouldn't have taken advantage. Seriously, I understand.'

'But you don't, Connor!' she said desperately. 'I don't want to marry David, I don't love David!'

Connor gave a gruff laugh.

'Then you'd best tell him that before he puts that giant sparkler on your finger.'

Her eyes opened wide.

'He's got... a ring?'

'Showed it all around the bar. Like a gull's egg it is.'

Kate took a breath, her legs unsteady beneath her. 'He bought me a ring?' she breathed.

He nodded glanced back towards the church.

'I should think Declan will be pleased.'

'But Connor, David...'

He shook his head and gently took her hands in his. 'Be happy, Kate O'Riordan,' he said, his eyes soft. 'That's all I wish for you.'

Then he turned and walked quickly down the path, leaving Kate standing among the stones in the rain.

Chapter 24

Ryan was late; he was always late. Connor sheltered under the narrow lych gate at the front of the church, peering through the sheets of rain towards the coast road. Where *was* he? Mind you, he hadn't given Ryan much notice and he'd needed to borrow the van from Jacky O'Donnell, who did like to talk, even by Clover Cove standards.

'Come on, come on,' he muttered. Connor resisted the urge to look over his shoulder back towards the church. He didn't want Declan spotting him and asking difficult questions like 'where are you off to?' and he didn't want to see Kate O'Riordan again.

Because if he did, he knew he'd lose his nerve and go back to her. And she would break his heart again, just like Ciara all over again.

He pushed his wet hair back anxiously and closed his eyes, trying not to think of Kate, trying to blank it all out. Trying not to think of the look on her face as her American boyfriend had come running out of that chopper. The shock, the embarrassment. The shame. The way she had dropped his hand and fallen into David's embrace. The way she had avoided his eye on the walk back to the village, as David had jabbered away, telling her how much he'd missed her back in New York and how he'd swung some deal with the Ross Oil bigwigs and now they could be together all the time.

But Connor couldn't help it. He turned to steal a look back at the church, hoping, praying to see her standing there. The churchyard was empty again. No Kate, no Declan, just stones and moss and the church with its wide arched door, just waiting for all the confetti and the wedding snaps. The nuptials of Kate O'Riordan and David Whatever-his-name-was. Connor instinctively knew David was the kind of man who would hold the ceremony in Clover Cove: it made sense from a business point of view. There was nothing the village liked more than a wedding and it would cement the happy couple's position – and the Ross Oil project – right at the heart of the Cove.

'Don't be a sore loser,' wasn't that what he'd said to Kate last night? Maybe Kate and David *were* in love; who was he to say otherwise? He barely knew the girl. He gave a rueful smile as he thought of her sitting there on that clifftop, the wind ruffling her wet hair. *Ah, but there was something about that girl, wasn't there?* Something beautiful and real. Da would have loved her too.

A horn parped and Connor turned to see Ryan waving, leaning out of the window of Jacky's bright yellow van. 'Are you coming, or are you going to sit there admiring the view?' he called.

Connor snorted and made a dash for the van. How could he be gloomy when his little brother never took anything seriously?

Ryan leant across to open the passenger door – the handle on that side had been missing for years – and

Connor slid inside. Ryan threw a holdall at him. 'As requested. One change of socks, a razor and a toothbrush.'

'Thanks,' said Connor, looking inside the bag and pulling out a folding umbrella and a tin of Guinness with a quizzical look.

'Irish survival kit,' said Ryan, crunching the gears as he turned the van around. 'So where to?'

'Anywhere but here,' said Connor. 'South. But take the hill road, I don't want to see the castle.'

Ryan glanced at him, but didn't say anything. He gunned the engine, fought a skid and turned out onto the road.

'So it's an adventure we're going on, is it?' he said, turning the windscreen wipers up a notch.

'Something like that.'

'Heading out into the wide blue yonder, just two brothers without a care in the world. Like Thelma and Louise, huh?'

Connor glanced at his brother.

'Didn't they end up dead?'

'Ah so. Bonnie and Clyde then?'

'Same thing.'

Ryan clicked his tongue. 'You're quite the ball of joy today, aren't you?'

He looked across. 'And what's brought this on, may I ask?'

'Brought what on?'

'This,' said Ryan, gesturing through the windscreen. 'The open road. I've been banging on about leaving the Cove for years and you've always told me I was an idiot.'

'You *are* an idiot. But now I'm going with you,' said Connor. 'We can be eejits together. But this way I get to watch over you, keep you out of trouble.'

Ryan laughed. 'Keeping out of trouble? Where's the fun in that?'

He ground the gears, shifting down as the road rose towards the coast. The van's cab was high enough that Connor could see over the wall down to the sea, rolling under the storm clouds. Ryan was right: he'd talked about running away for so long. All those maps he'd studied as a boy, all those postcards and magazine clippings of faraway places he'd collected and pasted onto his bedroom wall. And right now, he couldn't think of a single place he wanted to go.

He heard Ryan take a deep breath, then let out a growl of frustration. Yanking the steering wheel, Ryan pulled over at the side of the road, pulling on the handbrake with a jerk.

'What are you doing?' asked Connor.

'It's this American girl, isn't it?'

'What? No!'

Ryan laughed. 'You always were a terrible liar, brother. So her man from New York has come across in his flying machine and swept her off her feet, is that it?'

Connor didn't answer and Ryan raised a hand towards the van's roof.

'I'm not a *complete* idiot, Con. I could hardly miss a shiny helicopter landing on the cliffs. You don't need to be Columbo to join the dots. So she's gone back to him, is that it?'

Connor looked at him, then blew out his cheeks. 'Alright, yes. David – that's his name. David waltzed into the bar and announced to everyone they were getting married. Though Kate said...' He shook his head. 'Ah, it doesn't matter what she said. Fella's got an engagement ring the size of a fist.'

'Ah, and you don't think you can compete?'

'Of course I can't compete, Ryan!' said Connor in frustation. 'This David has money and a career and – and a bloody helicopter! He's American, she's American. What can I offer? And anyway, they're getting married.'

'Are they?'

'What do you mean?'

'Well it looks to me as though that's up to you, brother.'

'Me?'

Ryan let out a laugh.

'Con, the way you look at that girl – and the way she looks at you.' Ryan shook his head. 'Man, if I could just have a girl look at me like that once...' He gave a long whistle. 'That would be something.'

He twisted in his seat, facing Connor.

'She looks at you like Mam used to look at Da.'

'What? Come on.'

'It's true. And isn't that what you've been wanting all these years? Your soppy romantic ideal of love? Isn't that why Ciara broke you in two?'

Connor glanced at him, then looked away.

'Don't talk about her. Come on, let's go, I'm not here to be psychoanalyzed.'

'Well maybe it *is* time you talked to a shrink, brother,' said Ryan. 'Ever since Ciara...'

'You be quiet!' Connor roared, curling his hand into a fist, 'You mention her again and...'

'And what?'

He yelled again in frustration and jerked the door open, grabbing his bag.

'Fine, I'll walk.'

Connor jumped down from the van and slammed the door, walking out into the rain. Ryan knew exactly which buttons to press, he always had. That was how it worked with siblings; they knew your weaknesses intimately. But he was wrong about part of it at least. Connor wasn't chasing his parent's version of romantic love. He wasn't so starry eyed that he believed Rose and Cormac's relationship had been something out of a Disney movie. Connor could remember them screaming at each other, he could remember pots and pans being thrown in the kitchen, he could remember his father storming off along the cliff tops, just like Connor himself did when he needed space. But he remembered good times too. Lots of them. He remembered Mam and Da together behind the bar, he remembered all the laughter and the kisses and the warmth, an open happiness that had enveloped Connor and Ryan and Luke and Marion and most of the Cove into the bargain. Who wouldn't want that for themselves?

He heard footsteps and turned, holding up his bag defensively. It wouldn't be the first time an argument with his hot-headed brother came to blows.

'Hey, hey!' said Ryan, patting the air. 'Just slow down, will ya? Hear me out.'

Connor looked off down the road. It was a long way to Port Quinn and it didn't look like the rain was going to stop any time soon.

'Go on then,' he shrugged. 'Say your piece.'

'Look, maybe I shouldn't have mentioned Ciara, that's your business. But this Kate, she's real you know? She's not...'

Ryan trailed off.

'She's not what?'

'A ghost, Con.'

'A *ghost*?'

Ryan smiled sadly.

'Ciara, your great love. She's like some hazy phantom; not quite real.'

'Oh, she was real,' said Connor, his mind flashing onto a

far-off evening on top of the cliffs, wrapped together in a blanket. 'She was real, believe me.'

'The girl was real, sure. But the girl left, Con. The ghost was what was left behind and it's easy to love something like that, some wafty thing in a dress. Real people are harder to love.' He looked meaningfully at Connor. 'Because they irritate the cuss out of you.'

Connor smiled for a moment, then felt it fade.

'Maybe you're right; about Ciara I mean. Maybe I've built her up as some tragic lost love. Lord knows it hurt when she left, maybe I was just protecting myself.'

'Maybe?'

'Alright, so I did. But this Kate... maybe she's the same, you know? I think I saw what I wanted to see in her, made her into something she's not.'

'And maybe you didn't, Con. Maybe she is the real thing. Are you going to run away from her too?'

More buttons being pressed. He pulled his coat tighter.

'I didn't run away from Ciara!' snapped Connor. '*She* was the one who ran away.'

'Sure, sure. And you haven't just been using Clover Cove as a comfort blanket to hide under. I mean, everyone's been saying how upbeat and open you've been these past two years.'

He couldn't help laughing at that one. And Ryan was right, there had been a time when Connor James had seized life by the scruff of the neck. He'd planned to travel the world, live and laugh and make his mark. But somehow it hadn't happened.

'Okay, so you're right. I've been stewing in misery.' He turned and began to stride back towards the van. 'Well now I'm going – we're going.'

He pulled the van door open and threw his bag in.

'Come on, let's hit the road. It's time.'

Ryan clambered into the cab next to his brother and looked at him. 'You sure about this, Con?'

Connor looked out to sea, watched it heave, dark and deep. Then he leant over and clapped his brother on the shoulder.

'I'm sure,' he said. 'Let's roll.'

Chapter 25

Kate leant against the church wall and tried to control her breathing. How could he? How could he just *leave*? Hidden by the branches of a knotted old yew tree, water dripping down her back, she had watched Connor climb into the van and she had seen it jerk back and forth in a stuttering circle, turning back the way it came. Every second she had wanted to run across, throw herself in front, bang on the window, yell at him to get out, to stay.

But she hadn't. The van had crunched through the gears and driven away. It felt as though someone had torn something from her chest. *But why?* Why did she feel this way? Connor James was the enemy. He'd fought her every step of the way, he'd been rude and offensive and...

He had saved her.

'Oh no.' Kate bit back a sob, her hands over her eyes. She tipped her head back, feeling the ancient stone behind her, sucking in air, trying to get control.

Now she had to go back into the bar and face those people – and David.

David.

How could he do that, how could he tell everyone they were engaged? How could someone be that... arrogant? She shook her head. That was like asking 'how could that bull be so careless in that china shop?' Arrogant was David's defining characteristic and if she was honest, it was that confidence, his whirlwind of self-assurance that she had been swept along by when they had first begun dating, until she had finally realized that David was all surface, all polish and sleight-of-hand. He was like opening a well-wrapped present covered in bows and ribbons and finding an empty box inside. And now she had to go back there and... what? Bawl at David, point out in front of the packed bar that he hadn't even had the decency to pop the question first? That wouldn't exactly help the tidal project, would it? Did she really want to turn the community against the Ross Oil man, however much of a jerk he was? Kate pushed her wet hair out of her eyes.

'Why am I thinking about the job right now?' she whispered. This was her *life*. Even the most hardline human resources department would draw the line at asking an employee to get married just to make a project go smoothly. No, she had to go in there and speak to David, however awkward it was. Kate clambered past the rusty gate and walked slowly back along the muddy path to the gap in the hedge. She was soaked through already; she wasn't sure she could get any more wet.

An engagement ring, she thought with an ironic smile. If David had produced it three weeks ago when they had met at Dino's, their favorite restaurant in SoHo, she was almost certain she would she have gushed 'Yes! Yes please!' to appreciative applause from the other diners. After all, David was right about one thing: it would be a good strategic move for her career. As one half of the Ross Oil power couple, Kate was sure she could easily scoot up the ladder to board level and it wasn't too much of a stretch to see David as a future CEO. But picturing that life, even as a 'what if?' daydream, made something in Kate's heart ache. Only a month ago, an engagement would have felt like the first step towards her perfect life: an apartment on the Upper East, a house share in the Hamptons, a driver and a seat on some charity committee. Now? She felt like something was being snatched away.

Reluctantly, dragging her feet, Kate walked through the pub yard and up to the back door. Her hand was on the latch, just about to push through when she heard a voice on the other side. David's voice.

'Look, you know I can't talk now,' he said. A pause, then: 'I know that, but it's not private.'

Kate didn't need x-ray vision to know that David was on his cell phone. Typical: she'd spent the week waving her phone about near her bedroom window hoping for a single bar to appear, but David just strode in and got perfect reception.

'I can't,' David repeated and something about his tone – hushed, but forceful – made her stop and listen. 'I'm in a difficult situation here, you have to understand that,' he hissed. 'No, baby, I need to get back.'

Baby? Kate held her breath, her ears tingling.

'You *know* how I feel, but I need to stick to the plan. Just let me get this deal all tied up and then I can get rid of her.'

Kate's hand slipped over her mouth. *Get rid of her?* 'Her' as in 'me'?

David's tone changed as he said, 'Don't talk that way, baby.' He was practically purring. 'You know how hot it gets me when you talk like that. Just keep it warm and I'll be back real soon.'

Oh no, thought Kate, stifling a laugh. *The poor girl.*

'Look Ginny, I've got to go, your BFF will be back any moment.'

The smile immediately faded from her mouth. Ginny? *My Ginny*?

David laughed, the sound echoing in Kate's head.

'No, I don't think she'll want to be your bridesmaid when she finds out,' he said, chuckling. 'In fact, I think we might need to employ security at the wedding.'

Kate stumbled away from the back door, blindly running for the gap in the hedge, turning away from the church and the village, following the overgrown path up and up, just wanting to get away, her breath only coming in sobs. She vaguely felt branches and bushes pulling at her, but she kept going up the steep climb, out onto the clifftops, the wind whipping at her hair, until she was standing at the edge, staring out at the steel grey sea.

The storm was moving away now, the sky brightening, and Kate pressed two hands over her face, trying to erase the horror, the betrayal. *David and Ginny?* It couldn't be; she must have misheard, misunderstood. But she hadn't; Kate knew in her heart it was true. It certainly explained a lot. Ginny had been the one who had encouraged her to split up with David when he had co-opted her project. It had been Ginny who had suggested it would be best to 'make a clean break' and leave David behind. And if she was honest, hadn't Kate always had a sneaking suspicion? Little sideways glances, arm-touching, laughing too hard at David's lame jokes when they'd been out as a group...

Kate blew her cheeks out, feeling the sting of the sea on her skin. Did it matter? Did any of it matter now? Kate was done with Ireland and she was done with Ross Oil and if she was honest, she was done with Manhattan too. She couldn't go back, even if she wanted to.

And worst of all, she couldn't go back to Connor's either, could she? She couldn't sit there with everyone looking at her: Raff grinning, Orla giving her the thumbs up, everyone whispering about the ring, looking at David, thinking what a fine catch he was, pretending everything was fine.

Even his proposal was a lie! Kate could hardly believe it. David was as shallow as a motel sink, but she hadn't guessed he'd stoop that low.

Kate turned to look back at the Cove and the curve of the headland beyond the beach. It was strange to think she had never been up this side of the village before, but then Kate reflected that she had only been in Clover Cove a matter of days; it felt much longer. It was easy to see why Connor had been so protective of the village. It was so beautiful, but so delicate, like one big wave might sweep it all out to sea. The only solid thing was the chapel. Squat, hewn from slabs of grey rock, it looked like it had always been there since the headland had risen from the waves.

Kate walked over, crossing her arms. The rain had stopped, but she was still bone cold. Up close, the chapel was bigger than it looked from the beach. *Well, obviously.* She tried the latch on the door. Kate had a vague recollection of having read that they didn't lock churches in Ireland. Something about a tradition of being able to shelter from the Viking raiders or something. They certainly didn't leave churches unlocked in New York. The door swung inward and to her surprise, Kate saw Bishop Ray standing inside.

'Miss O'Riordan,' he said. Not quite a smile, certainly not welcoming, but Kate was freezing and she wasn't in the mood to be intimidated. She stepped into the chapel, rubbing her upper arms.

'It's cold out there, isn't it?' said the Bishop. Kate frowned at him, wondering if he was referring to her situation rather than talking about the weather. She nodded.

'Didn't expect anyone to be here,' she said, her teeth chattering. The priest clucked his tongue and pulled a blanket from the back of a pew. 'Here, put this around you. We provide them for the congregation; gets draughty up here.'

Kate wrapped it around her gratefully. 'I didn't know it was a working chapel.'

'Oh yes, it's been in constant use since the time of the saints,' said Ray, indicating a carved stone inscription on the wall.

'I don't read Gaelic,' she said.

'Neither do I, not much anyway,' said the old man. 'But roughly speaking, it says the chapel was built in 1492 and declares this spot and all the land and sea within man's gaze to be the kingdom of the Lord, so long as men worship here.'

'1492? Isn't that the year Columbus sailed the ocean blue?'

'Very good Miss O'Riordan.'

Kate shrugged.

'One of the few bits of history you need to know in American schools.'

'Well, we stick to the tradition of the carving and hold a service here once a fortnight, but as you can see, we struggle to fit more than a few dozen worshipers inside. At Christmas, however, we have a procession up from the church in the village and hold midnight mass in the open air.' He smiled. 'Which is fine as long as we don't get snow.'

Kate saw that he had spread some old papers out on the table in front of him.

'Oh, I hope I'm not interrupting anything.'

'Not at all. Just going over some documents we keep here. You don't know anything about law, do you?'

'American law, yes. It was my major in college; how I came to be working for Ross Oil in fact.'

'Oh?'

'Ironically, I wrote a term paper about a class action against Ross Oil in Alaska. It caught the eye of Leo Stern, the CEO, who offered me a post-grad internship. I guess I never left.'

'Well then you might be interested. Perhaps you'd care to look?'

Ray gestured to the yellowing paper in front of him. It looked ancient, written in scrolling ink; Kate could imagine a priest hunched over it hundreds of years before, scratching with a quill by lamplight.

'It's a beautiful artefact, but I don't understand the words.'

'Oh it's English – old English, anyway – with a little Latin thrown in, much like modern legal documents.'

Kate bent over the paper, squinting: 'Does that say *mare liberum*? It means "The High Seas," doesn't it?'

'Very good. Your boss would be proud.'

Kate frowned.

'My boss?'

'Oh, I assumed the chap who flew in on the gyrocopter was this Leo, your boss?'

'Oh. Different boss – or ex-boss, I should say.'

'Ex? Has something happened?'

'You could say that, Bishop. More of a personal nature than professional.'

He looked at her with his old eyes.

'Ah. I think I understand. So am I to assume this means you'll be leaving us?'

'Yes, I think so. I wish I wasn't, but...'

Kate turned away in embarrassment as tears began to roll down her cheeks. 'Sorry,' she said, 'I don't usually get like this. It's just... been a long week.'

'There now,' said the priest, coming around the table and laying a gentle hand on Kate's shoulder. 'Come and sit here by the window,' he said, producing a crisp handkerchief from nowhere. 'I have a flask of coffee here. Proper coffee, none of this instant nonsense. I'm thinking you'll appreciate it, being an American and all.'

Kate sat in the window seat and wiped her nose on the handkerchief. 'Thank you, Bishop. Actually, how do you address a bishop? Is it your Grace?'

'That's an archbishop. Technically, it's 'my Lord', but I don't believe anyone has used that in the years I've been a bishop. People still call me Father, which as I'm sure you know is incorrect, but between you and I, I don't mind. The Church of Ireland still considers itself Catholic, did you know that? So it's a tradition that fits.'

He poured her a cup of black coffee and handed it across.

'I think you're nicer than most people think, Bishop.'

The old man chuckled.

'Yes, I know people see me as hardline and I suppose I do have rather old-fashioned views, but the old tea-and-sympathy routine is pretty much 90% of the job. If I didn't care, it'd be a tough old life. And I do care about this place, about Clover Cove and all the people in it, even if we do have a disagreement every now and then.'

Kate nodded and sipped her coffee, wrapping her hands around it, grateful for the warmth.

'So these tears, Katherine. I take it they'll be for Connor James, not this new man in his flying machine?'

'Connor?' she coughed. 'But... how did you know?'

'Ach, no magic involved. As I say, I'm old enough to

have seen a few things. I overheard you bickering together after the village meeting in the church. Reminded me of myself and my wife, back when we were courting. Young love isn't like they write it in the television romances, Kate. It's passion and flame. Or it should be.'

Kate opened her mouth to speak, but couldn't think how to explain it all.

'I tried to tell him how I felt, but he...' she felt the tears coming again. '...He just walked away.'

Ray nodded.

'He's a good man, but he's been hurt.'

'A good man?' Kate repeated, 'I got the impression you disliked each other.'

'Can't speak for Connor, but I happen to think he's grown into a fine young man. Without Connor James, Clover Cove would have fallen apart years ago.'

Kate's surprise must have shown, because Ray smiled.

'Ah, we butted heads, sure. Same with his Da, but I think the Good Lord sent Connor to help the village. And I think he sent you to help Connor.'

Kate gave a nervous laugh.

'Me? Really?'

'Kate, you get to my age, you realize that true love is a rare thing. And when it comes along, you have to grab it with both hands and never let it go, however difficult it seems.'

'But he walked away, Father. I mean Bishop. I mean...'

'You know about Ciara? His old girlfriend? He loved her, but she didn't feel the same. So I imagine young Connor's scared of going down that road again. We're only human, Kate. You burn your hand, you don't want to put it into the flame again.'

'So what do I do?'

The old man shrugged.

'Like I say, it's not easy. I'd guess you have to go and tell him he's being a gombeen.'

'I'm sorry... gombeen?'

'A spanner, a flute, an eejit.'

Kate smiled.

'Ah. But there's a big problem. I can't stay. My ex-boss, David, has done a deal with Sir Charles, so the Ross Oil development is going ahead.'

'Is it now?'

'I'm afraid so. I wish it wasn't. Which probably sounds crazy given that's why I came here but...'

'But the Cove gets into your soul, doesn't it?'

She nodded sadly.

'Hmm. Well, ask and ye shall receive, Katherine,' said the priest, standing. 'Come back and look at these papers.'

Kate followed him back over to the table. 'As you'll be aware, the grapevine is faster than fibre optic in this village,' he went on, 'So I'd heard about the new Ross Oil deal with Charles Balcon – that's why I was up here.'

She frowned down at the document.

'What is this?'

'Documents relating to land rights, an official version of that inscription on the wall, if you like. See this seal? It's King James I, so it's old – 1607 – but as you'll be aware, in law, old is gold.'

Kate looked at it, fascinated. 'It's really that old? What's it say exactly?'

'The land on which this chapel is built was granted to the church by the crown. You've heard about the Gunpowder Plot?'

'Some guy in a big hat tried to blow the king up, right?'

'Exactly. So King James was keen for the protestant church to control as much of his kingdom as possible. That's why he granted this land to the church.'

Kate looked up and out of the window towards the cove.

'How much land is included?'

'All of it.'

'*All* of it?'

'As the inscription says: as far as man can see.'

'But Charles Balcon owns the land south of the cove, doesn't he?'

The old priest tapped the paper. 'Precisely,' he smiled. 'He owns all the *land* above the beach. The church owns the beach and the cliffs, all the way to the next county.'

Kate frowned. 'But I don't see...'

'Can you read this?' He pointed to a line and Kate bent over it.

'*Cuius est solum eius est usque ad coelum et ad infernos,*' she read haltingly.

'Ad coelum'? she repeated, looking up at the Bishop. 'I recognize that phrase. Doesn't it mean 'up to the sky?'

'Yes, my reading is, 'Whoever owns the soil, owns it all the way up to heaven and down to hell', or to put it another way, the ground and the air. Which means...'

Kate gasped.

'Which means Ross Oil can't run pipes or cables onto Sir Charles' land without the church's permission!'

'Which it will not give. Not while I'm bishop anyway.'

She threw her arms around his neck and kissed him.

'That's amazing news!'

'It is? But doesn't that mean you'll be leaving?'

'Depends. I need to ask someone something first.'

She opened the door and ran. Across the cliffs, down the muddy path, the out-sized wellies skidding once or twice, but keeping her feet. Finally, she dashed up the path and through the back door, into the bar. It was even more full than usual, presumably because most of the village had 'popped in' to see The Man From Ross Oil. David was holding court on the far side and Raff was standing behind the bar, just finishing pouring a pint of Guinness.

'Ah Miss Kate, just in time for that drink, eh?' he said, placing it on the bar.

Kate looked down at it. 'Actually, yes,' she said. 'Thanks, Raff.'

She picked it up and strode across to David, who was still sitting next to Danny Brennan, the reporter.

'Hey hon,' he smiled. 'I was wondering where you'd got to, I was just telling my friend Danny here...'

But Kate stopped him by placing the pint of Guinness down in front of him with a thump.

'Here "hon," I got you a drink. And I hear you have something for me.'

He looked at her, then across at Raff. The fisherman gave David a long wink.

'Ah, I see. Well, I was hoping for a more intimate moment, but...' he said, putting his hand into his jacket pocket. It was a Hugo Boss suit, Kate knew. He'd had it specially tailored with an Italian silk lining. Appearances were very important to David. He pulled out a deep red ring box and opened it. All the women in the bar gasped. Connor had been right: the diamond was huge. It twinkled and shone and for a moment, Kate was mesmerized, like she was staring into the eyes of a cobra.

'Kate O'Riordan,' he said, going down on one knee and holding the ring out towards her, 'Will you marry me?'

She felt rather than heard a collective intake of breath. For a second, everything seemed to hang in the air. Then Kate picked up the pint of Guinness and poured it over David's head. Gasping, David pinwheeled backwards, feet slipping on the beer and going down flat on his back, ring flying through the air. Kate reached out and caught it.

'No David,' said Kate. 'I will not marry you.'

'Why...' he coughed, 'Why not?'

'Because you're a spanner. And a flute. And an eejit. Oh, and because you've been playing footsie with my best friend behind my back.'

An appalled groan rippled around the bar. They were loving this. So, if she was honest, was Kate.

She looked down at the ring. 'I will, however, be keeping this. Or rather,' she walked back and handed it to Raff. 'I will donate it to the community of Clover Cove. I'm sure something this big will buy a clinic or a community hall. How's that sound, David?'

From the floor, David glared at her, then at the ring. He knew he couldn't say no if there was any hope of keeping the village on side. He nodded. 'Sure,' he said.

A big cheer rang around the bar.

'Oh, by the way David. I've just come from a meeting with Bishop Ray,' said Kate when the cheers had subsided. 'You haven't met the Bishop yet, have you? Well he's very... principled, isn't that right?'

She turned to the crowd, who all nodded, muttering 'aye,' 'that's right,' and 'hard man, God love him.'

'Anyway, it turns out the *bishop* controls access to the land around Clover Cove, not your friend Sir Charles. So it looks like you're going to have to go back to New York empty-handed.'

She turned to address the crowd.

'And to you, people of Clover Cove, I think I owe you an apology. Sorry for tempting you with speedboats and hot tubs you don't need. Sorry for even dreaming about changing the beauty of this cove. And sorry for making a mess on the floor of your pub.'

There was a pause, then Raff cleared his throat. 'Ah, that's grand, I've got a mop,' he said. 'And it's been a pleasure to have you here.'

Kate turned to the fisherman.

'Raff, where's Connor?'

'Connor? Oh, sorry Kate. I thought you knew. He's gone.'

Kate felt something heavy turn over in her stomach.

'Gone?'

Raff looked uncomfortable.

'Jacky O'Donnell was in earlier. Ryan borrowed Jacky's van. They're heading south.'

'South? South where?'

'Cork? Kinsale? That's where I'd go.'

'But you don't know? Didn't he say?'

Raff raised his eyes towards the bar and Kate glanced back. Of course they were all listening. All part of the entertainment. Even David was looking interested. Throwing a glare towards the pub, Raff took Kate's arm and led her to the back.

'Look Kate, I don't want to be the bearer of bad tidings, but I got the impression Connor was going because...'

'Because what?'

'Because of you, Miss Kate. Because he thought yon fella in there – your David – *was* your David. I mean, he told us all you were practically engaged. We didn't know about...the problems. I guess Con just wanted to get away.'

Kate curled her hands into fists; she wanted to scream. She wanted to go back in there and pour that beer over David's head all over again.

'*When* did he go Raff?'

'When he left here. You followed him out, didn't you?'

'Oh no.'

That meant when she stopped him in the churchyard, he was on his way. Out of her life. *Really* out of her life. Forever.

'That was half an hour ago.'

'Sure. Although...'

'Although what?'

'Well, Jacky was saying his van isn't in the best nick and the starter's been giving him all kinds of gip...'

Kate was out the door and running across the square before Raff had finished speaking. She *couldn't* be this unlucky, could she? She couldn't have found Connor and Clover Cove, only to have them both snatched away at the last minute. God *couldn't* be that cruel. She ran out into the road, heading south, her wellington-clad feet flapping and wobbling, but she kept going, heart racing, breath ragged in her throat. Perhaps the van had broken down, perhaps it had thrown a flat. She had to try. As she ran, Kate cursed all those evenings she'd skipped the gym to work late, she cursed David, she cursed the dumb luck that had brought her here, only to have it all thrown back in her face.

Kate was panting now, her legs complaining, but she could see the rise in the road now and she forced one last burst, her mind's eye picturing the van sitting in a lay-by, Connor standing by the open hood, kicking a tire in frustration.

She skidded to a halt, bent over, whooping air in and out. The road was empty, so was the lay-by. Not a van, not a car. Nothing but empty tarmac. He had gone.

'No,' she groaned. 'No!' Hands on hips, she walked on, trying to catch her breath, trying not to feel the aching in her heart that wasn't anything to do with her cardiovascular system. *Why?* Why hadn't she told him exactly how she felt when she'd had the chance? Why? *Because he didn't let me!* She thought angrily. Because he's so irritating! So self-absorbed. Because he thought...

'Because he thought you were marrying David.'

That was why. And Kate couldn't really blame him for that. If she had discovered that Connor was engaged to some pretty, rich, successful woman with a helicopter, she would probably have walked away too.

Just then, Kate came to another of those stiles crossing the wall on the seaward side of the road. A leprechaun ladder. *Ha.* And a tilting wooden sign pointed westwards with the just-visible carved words 'Sleagh Castle'. Still puffing, Kate pulled herself up and over, walking down the sloping field towards the sea. It was the field she and Connor had crossed that first morning on their way to Ironship Bay, when they had sat thigh-to-thigh and watched the swooping Kittiwakes and diving Cormorants. And it was where Connor had so effortlessly come to her rescue, where he had touched her face and told her he didn't want her to leave. Kate stopped, pressing a hand to her heart. *I don't want you to leave.* She closed her eyes, feeling the breeze on her face, heart beating in her ears as the sea and the cries of the gulls echoed up toward her.

'This so sucks,' she said. '*So* sucks.'

Shaking her head sadly, she jumped down onto the little hidden path Connor had led her to and began picking her way along. This, she supposed, really would be her last time to see that magnificent coast. Kate knew she would have to go back to New York and face whatever music was there to be faced. Would she lose her job? Probably. Although Leo liked her, pure economics would make him side with David, however badly he'd behaved. And if this episode had taught her anything, it was that she needed to move on. She had been at Ross Oil since college and while she had traveled the world and done amazing things, she wanted something more rooted, something with meaning, something like she had found here in Clover Cove. But she couldn't stay here, that was for sure.

Kate edged around an outcrop, looking down to where the waves were breaking. She had thought she would be frightened to come back here after her near-miss on the cliff, but she didn't; in fact it felt natural and familiar. She could see why Connor came here when he wanted to be alone. It wasn't lonely – how could it be with all this life teeming everywhere? – but at the same time there was enough wide-open space to let your thoughts roam free.

'Hey there.'

Kate almost screamed, grabbing hold of a tuft of grass and clinging to it.

'Connor!'

Relief flooded through her. *He was here! He was here!* Sitting on that flat rock, just like that first morning, the collar of his pea coat flipped up, his green eyes looking at her.

'I thought you'd gone, I thought...'

He shook his head. 'Couldn't do it. I've been running for too long. It's about time I started living. And however much it hurts, that's what I've got to do.'

'Connor, I need to tell you something.'

He shook his head, waved a hand.

'Ach, Kate. You don't want have to explain anything...'

'I want to stay,' she blurted out, cutting him off.

He frowned. 'Stay?'

She edged closer, until she was sitting next to him.

'Remember back up there on the cliff, you said you didn't want me to leave? Well here I am. If you want me to stay, I will.'

Connor shook his head.

'But you are staying, aren't you? With David?'

'That's what I was trying to tell you back there in the churchyard, David and I, we split up way before I got here. And there's no way on earth I'm marry that head-the-ball, not in a million years.'

Connor blinked at her.

'Head-the-ball?'

'It means butt-head, right?'

'Near enough. Where'd you get that expression from?'

'Bishop Ray.'

Connor burst out laughing.

'Well, it has been a strange day.'

He looked at her.

'So if you're not with David and you're not going to marry him in a million years, what are you going to do?'

'Thought I might hang around and watch the birds. What are you going to do?'

'This,' he said, bending to kiss her softly on the lips. Kate felt it tingle all the way down to her frozen toes. He made to pull away, but she held onto him, kissing him back. It was good. No, it was better than that. It was perfect.

'Wow,' she said, finally pulling back.

'I've been waiting a long time to do that,' smiled Connor.

Kate gave him a sidelong look.

'How long exactly?'

'Oh, from that first day.'

'What? I thought you hated me.'

'Whatever gave you that idea?' he smiled. 'It was your wind tunnels I disliked.'

'Wind tunnels? Tidal turbines, you mean?'

'Yeah. That.'

It was Kate's turn to laugh.

'Do you have any idea what this was all about?'

'Oh I know exactly what this is about,' said Connor, pulling her in for another kiss. And another.

Finally, they walked arm in arm back towards the village as Kate filled Connor in about Bishop Ray and David and the ring. Connor listened quietly, nodding and taking it all in. Just before they were about to cross the stile,

Connor stopped her and turned to face the view of Clover Cove.

'Sure, but it wouldn't be the same with poles and turbines and whatnot sticking out of it, would it?'

Kate sighed and slid an arm around his waist. 'No, I suppose not.'

'So what are you going to do, Connor? About the Cove, I mean?'

'Ah, we'll be grand. I'm thinking of expanding the spa.'

She smiled.

'Seriously though.'

Connor waved a hand vaguely.

'Your brains and my beauty, we'll work something out.'

'But what about...'

He stroked her hair. 'Hey, if we've got each other, it doesn't matter does it?'

'No,' Kate smiled, leaning her head against his shoulder. 'No, I don't suppose it does.'

* * *

Thanks for reading Love Comes to Clover Cove – I hope you enjoyed it!

If you'd like to be kept up to date on all the new releases and happenings in Clover Cove why not sign up for my Clover Cove newsletter over on Maggie-finn.com?

Other books in the Clover Cove series:

'A Secret in Clover Cove'

Tessa Drake has a secret. A secret that has kept the beautiful artist locked in her studio right on Clover Cove's lovely windswept beach. But secrets have a way of getting out and it doesn't help that she's fallen head over heels in love with the one man she shouldn't: investigative journalist Danny Brennan. Danny is her perfect man, he's clever and handsome, but he's also getting too close to the story. And Danny has his own dilemma: should he reveal a long-hidden scandal? It could kick-start his career, but might tear his family apart. Can Tessa find a way to mend her heart? And will Danny find the real truth; that sometimes love can overcome even the deepest secrets?

'The Little at Café at Clover Cove'

Molly Maguire's life is romantic enough: she makes delicious cakes and her café has the most beautiful view in Ireland, Clover Cove's windswept beach. So why would she need a man? Besides, Maggie has bigger problems. The café is failing and the bank is threatening to shut her down, which would mean heartbreak for Molly, especially as she has just fallen in love with a mysterious surfer.

If Maggie closes the café, she will have to leave Clover Cove and go back to work for her ex, handsome celebrity chef Marcus. Can Molly and her friends find a way to save the Little Café in Clover Cove? Or will she have to choose between true love and the future of Clover Cove itself?

'Snow Falls in Clover Cove'

Everyone loves Noah, Clover Cove's only policeman. He's handsome, charming and devoted to his job, keeping the quirky residents of Kiln County safe and happy, especially during Christmas, a time when burning turkeys and overheated families can lead to explosions. But this year, after an emotional few months, all Noah wants is a quiet Christmas break.

Heartbroken publishing executive Eliza needs to escape Los Angeles for the holidays – and postcard-pretty Clover Cove looks the perfect place - but when she meets Noah, she knows he is her second chance at love. But why is Noah determined to stay single? Can Eliza persuade Noah to open his heart and rediscover the magic of family and friends - and can they find their own happily ever after?

'A Love Letter from Clover Cove'

Clover Cove is a gorgeous Irish village full of warmth and sunshine, a place with feel-good romance around every corner. But when Orla Keane finds an unsigned love letter, the coastal community is turned upside down. Post mistress Orla is always the first to hear about every new love story in Kiln County, but when she finds the love letter, she is drawn into a romantic mystery. Who is the love letter from? Who is it to? Could it even have a link to her own failed romance with Aaron Garvey, the handsome local farmer with a poetic soul? To find an answer, Orla will have to choose between following her dreams or putting family and friends first, even if it means risking heartbreak all over again.

'Coming Home to Clover Cove'

Nicole Garvey loves her glamorous life in London, so going home to Clover Cove for the festive season makes her heart sink, until she runs into her first love Liam Daly and remembers why she fell head-over-heels for him the first time around.

But it seems as though Liam has other ideas. His roots in the village go deep and there is no way he is going to give up his idyllic life on the romantic West Coast, even if it means breaking Nicole's heart all over again. But this is Clover Cove, where magic can happen at any time of the year. Can Liam and Nicole find happiness even if it means a drastic change of plan?

Maggie-finn.com

Printed in Great Britain
by Amazon

85388505R10115